Praise
Carlton M

Also by Carlton Mellick III

CUDDLY
HOLOCAUST

CARLTON MELLICK III

ERASERHEAD PRESS
PORTLAND, OREGON

ERASERHEAD PRESS
205 NE BRYANT
PORTLAND, OR 97211

WWW.ERASERHEADPRESS.COM

ISBN: 1-62105-072-6

Copyright © 2013 by Carlton Mellick III

Cover art copyright © 2013 by Ed Mironiuk
www.edmironiuk.com

Printed in the USA.

AUTHOR'S NOTE

I was tasked with writing a title story for my next collection. A title story is the featured story, the one that brings the whole book together. It is meant to be the best, longest, and most engaging story in the collection—one that will make the book worth buying on its own. But most importantly it must have the best title, because it's the one the book is named after. The title story will make or break a collection, and the title of the title story will usually determine whether it sells at all.

When I put a collection together, I always write the title story last. It will be a story that rounds out the book and adds elements that I feel are missing from the other stories. The first thing I do is decide what I'd like to title the collection and then base a story after that.

It took me hours, if not days, of brainstorming to come up with a title for my third collection. The one that finally grabbed me was *Cuddly Holocaust*. It seemed perfect. All I needed to do was turn that title into a story and my collection would be complete.

But there was a problem: I can't write short stories. Ask anybody who knows me. Ask Jeff Burk, who regularly teases me whenever I say I'm going to write a short story. "Yeah, I'll believe it when I see it," he always says.

See, here's my issue: if I like what I'm writing I never want it to end. So my short stories often become novellas and my novellas often become novels. This only happens when I really like an idea. Of course, I almost always really like my ideas. Why bother writing a story if you don't really like the idea?

Cuddly Holocaust was such a case. I liked the idea so much that I couldn't end it where I originally planned. So it did not become a short story. In fact, it's too long to even be considered a novella. I just liked writing it too much to finish it. The result is a damn near epic tale set in an apocalyptic world populated by violent intelligent toys.

If anything wipes out humanity it might as well be toys. Toys are awesome. I've always dreamed of what it would be like if all my toys came to life. Either it would be fun and magical or completely terrifying. This book takes that latter idea and puts it on the apocalyptic scale. It ended up being one of the most disturbing books I've ever written, especially toward the end.

So here it is—my 38th book. It is being released side-by-side with my collection, which I did end up completing soon after Cuddly Holocaust. The title story is called Hammer Wives. It proved to me that sometimes I can complete a short story (as long as I shoot for writing a piece of flash fiction).

I hope you enjoy them both.

—Carlton Mellick III, 12/15/2012 4:07 pm

PART ONE

CHAPTER ONE

The doctor peeled off the last layer of human skin on Julie's arm and replaced it with a strip of soft black plushy fur.

"Panda bear, panda bear," the doctor sang to his patient, his scabby lips so wide Julie could see his crooked bronze teeth filled with grit and gum-blood. "Cute baby panda bear."

The doctor could spare no anesthetic on the operation, so even the air touching her skinless arm felt like serrated knives sawing at the exposed tissue.

The doctor continued singing in his raspy voice, "Eating up bamboo with the momma panda bear."

The young woman's screams reverberated through the metal halls of the underground bunker as the doctor sewed the piece of stuffed animal skin over the bloody patch of raw muscle. This was the sixty-seventh operation she had endured of this kind. Each one had been more painful than the last.

The doctor tossed a cotton panda arm over his shoulder, adding to the mountain of stuffed animal scraps behind him. They had gone through so many toys in order to transform her. It took her sixteen months of scouring the wasteland to find all of them, searching through the rubble of every crumbled building for miles around. There probably wasn't another stuffed panda toy left in the entire city. If the doctor didn't have enough plushy fur to finish the job, Julie didn't know what she would do.

"The momma panda bear loves the baby panda bear," sang the doctor. His eyes were far too big for his head, bugging out of the sockets at her. "And the baby panda bear loves the momma panda bear."

Julie couldn't take his raspy singing any longer.

"Could you shut the hell up?" she said in a high-pitched electronic voice. "You creep the hell out of me when you sing."

"*My* voice creeps *you* out?" said the doctor. He giggled.

"Listen to yourself."

One of the first operations the doctor performed on Julie was to remove her human voice box and replace it with that of a smart-toy. She hasn't had the voice of a human girl since that day.

"You sound like a child molester singing that song," Julie said in her inhuman tone.

"And you sound like a demented cartoon character," said the doctor. "You're giving everyone nightmares."

When the procedure was over, Julie rushed to the mirror to investigate her new black fluffy arm. It matched the rest of the fur covering her body. Only a few more operations and she would finally become a real plushy panda bear.

"Beautiful," said the doctor, admiring his work. "You look just like one of them."

"I don't want to just look like one of them," she said. "I want to become one of them."

She stripped off her raggedy clothes to see how she looked as a whole. Her skin was a patchwork of black and white fuzz. Her paws were firm and squishy. Her breasts were white puffy balls. The plushy skin had been grafted to ninety-three percent of her body. Only her face and some sections of her chest and armpits were left to go before she would be complete.

The doctor cleaned his tools in a blackened coffee can on the stove. "We'll start on the face next," he said. "That will be the most difficult part. It will require at least a dozen procedures."

"That many?"

"If you want to skip your face, I still have the mask," said the doctor. He opened a screeching metal drawer near the stove, revealing a panda face mask he had constructed months prior.

"I told you," she said, pulling her overalls back on. "It's not worth the risk. If I'm going to infiltrate them, my look has to be real."

The doctor tossed the panda mask back into the drawer. "Whatever you say, crazy girl."

She glanced one last time in the mirror and rubbed the fuzzy panda ears on the top of her head. It still hurt after the doctor scalped her last month, replacing her human head of hair with a hood of black and white fuzz.

"By the way," the doctor said. "You never told me..."

"What?" Julie said.

"Of all the stuffed animals you could have become, why did you choose a panda?" he said.

Julie bit into her blackened lip.

"I've always liked pandas," she said.

"But when's the last time you've seen a panda smart-toy out there?" he asked. "You would have fit in better as a teddy bear or bunny rabbit."

"Sometimes standing out is the best way to fit in," she said, rubbing sweat from her armpits with a handful of ashy cotton fluff.

Julie crawled beneath the Christmas tree to find her last present—the one with fairies and snowflakes on the wrapping paper.

"What did Santa bring you?" Julie's dad asked, standing behind her in his pine-scented pajamas.

Young Julie didn't respond, tugging at the heavy package, trying to get it out with all her might and nearly knocking the whole tree down in the process.

"Santa worked hard to get this one," said her father. "It was really expensive."

He held a reindeer-shaped mug of hot cocoa to his chin and blew at the steam rising through its antlers.

"Get me out of here," said a high-pitched voice from the package.

"What?" Julie said as she heard the voice, her eyes lighting up. The package began to move and shake on its own. "*What!*"

"Come on," said the voice. "I'm getting claustrophobic in here."

"What!" Julie screamed with excitement.

"Hurry up and open it," said her dad, sipping his cocoa.

"What's taking so long?" said the voice in the box. It had a cartoonish 1930s New York accent. "Are you slow in the head or something, kid?"

Julie ripped open the wrapping paper and saw a stuffed animal inside the box. It was alive and slapping at its plastic encasing, desperate to be freed.

"What is it? What is it?" Julie cried.

"It's a smart-toy!" said the father.

The toy crawled out of the box and shook out its fur.

"Ohmygawd! It's a panda! I love pandas!"

"Thanks, kid," said the stuffed animal, stretching its fluffy little limbs and taking deep breaths. "One more minute in there and I would have suffocated to death."

Then Julie swiped the panda into her arms and hugged it as tightly as she could.

"Hey wait a minute, what gives?" cried the panda bear. "Out of one prison and into the next!"

The toy flapped and wiggled in Julie's arms.

"You didn't actually get her one of those, did you?" said Julie's mother as she appeared behind them in the room. She was rubbing her head, way too hungover to be awake that early in the morning. "Jesus Christ…"

"It's what she wanted," said the father, smiling at his daughter's excitement.

"She's ten years old," said the mother. "She's too old for stuffed animals."

"But look at how cool it is," said the father. "I kind of wanted to buy another one for myself."

The mother shook her head. "Yeah, you would…" Then she went toward the kitchen to make another pot of coffee.

"What's its name? What's its name?" Julie asked.

"Don't ask me," said the father, pointing at the ruffle-faced toy. "Ask him."

"What's your name?" Julie asked the panda.

"Let me go and I'll tells ya," he said.

Julie let him go.

"Call me Poro," said the panda, wiping the girl's stink from his fur.

"Hi Poro, I'm Julie!"

"Yeah, great," Poro said.

Then the panda mumbled to himself, "I knew I'd get stuck with a flat chick…"

"I'll love you forever, Poro!" Julie cried, swiping the bear back up into her arms.

Young Julie played with her new friend nonstop the entire afternoon. Her parents sat on the couch and watched with amazement, bewildered by the advanced technology of the toy.

"How the hell is it able to talk like that?" Julie's mother asked her father. "It's like a real person."

"It practically is a real person," said the father. "It's programmed to have the intelligence of a human. It even has emotions."

"How can it have emotions?" she said. "It's just a computer program."

"Emotions are just programmed responses in both humans and computers," said the father. "If she's mean to the toy it will get sad. If she's nice to it the panda will love her back. She'll learn valuable social lessons interacting with it."

"I wish you would have talked to me before buying it," said the mother. "I don't know if I like the idea of that thing running around our house."

Poro tossed a pillow across the room at Julie. It missed the girl and stuck into the limbs of the Christmas tree. Then he laughed and pointed.

"It's going to be like living with a strange tiny man," said the mother.

"He's perfectly safe," said the father.

"Are you sure about that?"

"What's the worst that could happen?"

As Julie chased her new toy around the room, Poro tripped into an end table and knocked a goldfish bowl onto the linoleum floor. The glass shattered and sent the family goldfish flying.

"Say, who's the bozo who put that there?" said the panda, brushing the goldfish water from his fur.

The mother didn't have to say it, but she did anyway. "The worst that could happen?" She gave Julie's father a look. "Where do I begin?"

Then she rolled her eyes.

As Julie left the doctor's cabin, wiping blood and sawdust from her plushy coat, an explosion rumbled the bunker and knocked her off balance. A bolt of pain raced across her fur as her freshly-sewn arm slammed into the wall.

"What the hell was that?" Julie asked a soldier running past her in the corridor.

The young man turned back to respond but didn't stop moving, heading in the opposite direction of the noise. "They're here. They found us!"

Julie gripped her arm and pulled herself down the hallway toward the stairwell. There was a commotion up above—people screaming in a panic, running for their lives. Then the sound of gunfire.

"You bastards," she said, her electric voice echoing down the hallway. "I'm not ready yet. I was so damned close…"

She walked back toward the medical station. The doctor peeked his head through the door.

"You don't think you can finish the job in five minutes do you?" Julie asked him, pointing at her face.

The doctor shook his head.

"They're inside?" he asked. His face was even creepier when he was afraid.

"Yeah, sounds like it," she said.

Three soldiers fled down the hallway, away from the stairs. Two of them bled profusely. Judging by the expressions on their faces, they wouldn't have looked more traumatized if their foreskins had been split open by jagged rocks.

"How many of them?" Julie asked the soldiers.

"Too many," one of them cried, staggering as fast as he could.

The soldiers left a trail of blood so thick that Julie wondered how they could still have any remaining in their bodies.

Another said, "They're coming. Get out of here."

The doctor jumped back into his cabin.

As Julie followed him, bullets zipped past her shoulder. She looked back to see the soldiers torn to pieces by machine gun fire. They fell to the ground screaming, splashing into a puddle of their own blood.

The enemy marched down the steps into the corridor, led by a snarling tiger with an oversized terrycloth head. Just before closing the door behind her, Julie locked eyes with him. He was a seven-foot-tall stuffed animal walking on his hind legs, a demonic Tigger the Tiger with a bloodthirsty glare in his beady, black, ball eyes.

When they opened fire on her, Julie rolled sideways into the doctor's cabin, over her tender arm, then slammed and bolted the door. She only had enough time to move a single cabinet in front of the door before they were outside, clamoring to get in.

"Here," the doctor yelled at Julie, tossing her a shotgun.

The second she caught it, she pumped the shotgun and aimed it at the door. The stuffed animals outside roared, banging ferociously at the metal.

"It's reinforced steel," the doctor said, trying to talk over the banging noises. "They won't get in so easily."

The doctor was loading a heavy machine gun as he spoke.

"Where the hell did you get all this stuff?" Julie asked, crouching behind a row of cabinets.

The old creep had an entire arsenal beneath his operating table. Grenades, handguns, machetes, automatic rifles, he had it all.

"A lot of dead bodies come my way," said the doctor, positioning the weapon on top of the operating table, aiming for the doorway. "Whatever they got on them, I get to keep."

"The defense team could use that stuff," Julie said.

The old doctor spit across the grubby floor. "The defense team is probably dead by now."

Once he was ready, he nodded to Julie.

"Open the door," he said.

Julie looked at the banging door, then back at the doctor. "Are you crazy?"

"We need to take them out before reinforcements arrive," he said. "It'll catch them off guard."

Julie shook her fluffy head, but found herself complying. She moved the cabinet out of the way and prepared to unlatch the door.

"Open it when I say," said the doctor.

They listened to the banging noises outside of the door, following the rhythm of the bangs as the stuffed animals tried to ram the door down.

A second before the next bang, the doctor yelled, "Now!"

Julie opened the door and the giant stuffed tiger tumbled forward into the room. It tripped face-first into the barrel of the doctor's heavy machine gun.

The fluffy tiger's head was torn in half by an explosion of bullets. Electronic shrieks filled the room as the bullets ripped through two stuffed giraffes in the doorway.

"Get down," the doctor yelled.

Julie jumped behind the cabinets as she saw the grenades in the old creep's hands. He pulled the pins and tossed them into the hallway, then ducked behind the operating table. The remaining stuffed animals tried to run, but there was no cover in the hall.

The second after the grenades went off, the doctor grabbed a .45 magnum revolver. "Come on."

Julie followed him out into the hallway. There were six stuffed animal soldiers writhing on the ground out there, full of shrapnel, in shock from the blast. The doctor didn't hesitate for a second. He went from one animal to the next, putting massive bullet holes in their oversized fluffy heads.

"Get that one," the doctor yelled, pointing at a kitty cat that was crawling on its belly in the other direction.

Julie ran after the wounded stuffed animal and aimed her shotgun at the back of its head. The thing whimpered, sparks popping from its electronic voice box.

Before Julie pulled the trigger, the orange kitty cat looked up at her with wet blue eyes. Julie stepped back. There was something incredibly wrong with this one. Its eyes, they weren't plastic. They were the eyes of a human.

"Momma?" said the kitty cat.

As Julie pulled the trigger, the stuffed animal's face exploded, splattering brains across the floor and metal wall behind it. Julie nearly fell over when she saw the gore. It should have been filled with cotton and wires. Why did it have brains?

She looked at the other corpses in the hallway. Their bodies were covered in blood. Most of them also had human eyes within their plushy heads.

"Why are they bleeding?" Julie asked the doctor.

The old man examined one of them: a sheep with red fluid caked in its white fur. He dipped his finger through a bullet hole and pulled it out bloody.

"Interesting," the doctor said, ignoring the sound of screams and gunfire fading into the distance. "Help me move it out of the hallway."

They dragged the sheep's body into the doctor's cabin.

"How can it be bleeding?" Julie asked. "It's just a smart-toy."

The doctor took a scalpel from his boiling coffee can and stabbed it into the sheep's chest. He carved down its torso and then ripped open its belly, pulling out intestines like the guts of a Halloween pumpkin.

"What the hell?" Julie said.

The doctor found not only intestines, but a heart, lungs, a stomach, a circulatory system, even a brain.

"They're trying to become living beings," the doctor said, leaning over the pile of toy guts.

17

"What do you mean I'm just a toy?" Poro said to young Julie, standing on top of the coffee table and pointing a squishy paw at her. "I'm as alive as you is."

"Mommy says you're not really alive," Julie said. "You're just a really smart toy."

"Just because I'm all stuffing and wires instead of meat and blood don't mean I'm any less a living being," Poro said.

"But living beings have organs and stuff. You can't be alive unless you have organs."

"Who cares about organs? They get diseased. They rot. You have to take good care of them or else you get sick. They're just a pain in the ass if you ask me."

"It's just what mommy keeps saying."

"Well, forget her. That broad ain't know what she's talking about."

The panda bear sat on the edge of the table, crossing its arms and pouting. Julie looked down at her hands. She didn't want her friend to be too sad because of what she said.

"I think you're alive, Poro," Julie said, leaning forward to pet his shoulder.

The little panda smiled back at her and rubbed the top of her head.

"Thanks, squirt," he said. "I think you're alive, too."

When Julie's mother entered the room, she groaned loudly so that both of them could hear. "Julie, get that thing off the table."

"Who you calling a thing, lady?" Poro said.

The mother ignored the toy.

"Dinner's ready," she said. "Put that thing in your room and come eat."

"But Poro doesn't like being alone."

"Poro will be fine," said the mother, trying not to make eye contact with it. "Come eat."

Then she went back into the kitchen.

18

"Don't worry, squirt," Poro said to Julie. "While the rest of the family has dinner, I'll use the opportunity to sneak into your father's porn collection. That should keep me busy for a while."

Julie didn't know what he was talking about. She just smiled back, happy he didn't mind that he wasn't allowed at the dinner table.

The doctor continued examining the plushy corpse even though he knew he didn't have the time to linger.

"Grab as many weapons as you can carry," said the doctor. "We need to get out of here."

Julie went to the arsenal beneath the operating table and strapped ammunition belts around her waist and over her shoulders. The doctor filled a plastic container with the sheep's guts.

"What are you doing?" Julie yelled at him.

"Taking samples," said the doctor. "I need more time to study this."

"Let's just go."

"One second…" the doctor said, shoving his arm deep inside of the sheep's corpse. "I just need one more—"

The doctor's body exploded like a water balloon and pieces of him sprayed across the room. Julie fell back against the wall as sheep intestines rained down on her.

"What the hell was that?" Julie said to the splatter of gore in the room.

By the time she got back to her feet, she couldn't tell which corpse was human and which was the stuffed animal. Then there were three more explosions out in the hall. Then two more, blood spraying through the doorway in a red mist. It wasn't until the corpse of the stuffed tiger exploded in the middle of the room that Julie understood what was going on—the plushies were booby trapped. They must have had explosives implanted inside of their bodies, designed to go off ten minutes after death.

She couldn't understand the logic in filling soldiers full of explosives. What if they went off while they were still alive? What if one of them died while in close quarters with their own troops? It didn't make sense. But nobody really understood why the plushies did any of the things they did. Julie didn't have time to worry about it. She had to get out of there.

She looked down at the doctor's splattered corpse and allowed herself three seconds to mourn the old man. Although she wasn't very fond of him, he was the closest thing she had to a friend in that bunker. Nobody else would go anywhere near her once she started covering herself in panda fur.

"Thanks for everything, you old creep," she said.

As she turned away from the red mess of meat, the sound of footsteps echoed through the hallway. It was an entire army of plushy feet marching in her direction, coming to investigate the slaughter of their fallen comrades.

Julie looked over at the heavy machine gun, wondering if she should try to fight them off. But defeating them all by herself wouldn't be possible.

She went to the cabinet by the stove and retrieved the panda mask the doctor made for her. The second she placed it over her face, she was sure it wouldn't work, even with the black makeup she applied to her eyes, lips, and nostrils.

But then she examined herself in the mirror. The mask actually looked far more believable than she thought it would. It wasn't nearly good enough to work for long. Even the dumbest of smart-toys would recognize she wasn't one of them if they got within two feet of her face. But she had no other choice. The smart-toy army was just outside the room.

CHAPTER TWO

"I want to get rid of that thing," young Julie heard her mother saying to her father outside the kitchen.

"Why?" said the father. "Julie loves that toy."

"The thing creeps the hell out of me," said the mother. "And he's got the personality of a perverted truck driver. This morning he was hiding in the bathroom while I was taking a shower, and do you know what he said to me when I caught him?"

The father shrugged. "What?"

"He said 'Nice rack, toots,'" said the mother, trying to imitate Poro's accent. "Is that really the kind of toy we want around our daughter?"

"He's harmless," the father said. "It's just the personality he was programmed with. It's meant to be cute."

"He's not cute. He's vulgar. I want him out of this house."

"It would break Julie's heart."

"I don't care. She's just a kid. We'll buy her another stupid toy."

When Julie heard her say that, she ran into the dining room and yelled at them, "You're not taking Poro away! You can't!"

"Goddammit," the mother said, groaning. "You heard all of that?"

"He's my Poro," Julie cried. "I love him!"

"We'll get you a new toy," said her mother. "Anything you want."

"I don't want anything else," Julie said. "I love Poro. When I grow up, we're going to get married and be together forever."

"Married?" said the mother, laughing. "He's just a stuffed animal."

"No, he's alive," Julie said. "He's alive! He's alive!"

Then she barricaded herself in her room with Poro.

"What has gotten into her?" said the mother.

"I told you," said the father. "She loves that toy. Imagine how you'd feel if your parents tried to take away your puppy when you were a kid."

"That's different," said the mother. "Puppies are cute."

"That panda's her best friend. Take him away and she'll hold it against you for the rest of her life."

The mother just fumed.

"This is all your fault," she said. "You never should have gotten her that stupid thing."

"You're the only one who hates him," said the father.

"It's his behavior that I hate," she said.

"Well, maybe you should try talking to him," said the father.

"I'm not talking to a stupid toy," she said.

"Who knows, you might be able to reason with it."

Then the father went back to the kitchen and stuffed a toaster strudel in his mouth.

When the plushy soldiers arrived in the doorway, Julie just ignored them, piling guns on the operating table as if she were just doing what she was supposed to be doing. She knew her best chance would be to remain calm and keep busy. Reacting to them in any way was the worst thing she could do.

The leader of the group was a massive teddy bear, too large to even fit through the doorway. His eyes scanned the room and then locked on Julie. He just stared at her for a while, as if she didn't belong.

"What happened here?" asked the teddy bear.

Julie placed a few more weapons on the table before responding. She made sure not to make eye contact, even for a second.

"I found them this way," Julie said. "All dead."

Her electronic voice was perfect. If all they heard was her voice they would never suspect her of being human. But still, the bear seemed suspicious. He kept staring, as if waiting for her to break character.

"We don't collect supplies until after the floor has been cleared," said the bear.

"The floor is clear," Julie said.

"I'll decide when the floor is clear," said the teddy bear.

He glared at her a little longer. Julie realized that he wasn't at all suspicious of her being human, but was suspicious of her being an insubordinate that wasn't following orders.

"Just get all of that topside," said the bear. "Now."

Then he told his troops, "Move out."

Julie never looked at the bear's face. She only saw his massive brown form within her peripheral vision. She hoped she wouldn't have another run in with him again. Getting singled out by an officer would be the quickest way to end the deception.

When she was finally alone, she backed up and took a deep breath. She didn't leave the room until after the sound of marching footsteps faded to silence.

"What's up your ass now, lady?" Poro asked Julie's mother.

They were in her office. Julie's mother wanted to have a word with the stuffed animal, talk to him about his behavior. Just as the father suggested, she was going to try to reason with him. But she just felt silly trying to have a serious conversation with a toy.

"I just want to have a talk with you," said the mother.

"You sure you don't want to fool around?" said the panda, gently rubbing the mother's calf. "Your husband won't be home for hours and I'm aching for some action over here."

The mother gasped and pulled away from him.

"What the hell's wrong with you?" she cried.

"I'm just pulling your leg, lady," said the panda. "Don't get so bent out of shape. I don't even have the proper equipment down here." He pointed at his fluffy crotch. "They give me the sex drive of a horned up frat boy but no tools to do the job with. What's up with that?"

"That's what I want to talk to you about," said the mother, sitting down at the desk. "Your behavior. I find it completely inappropriate."

The panda hopped up into a chair facing her. "But I'm just being me."

"But I don't want your lewd behavior around my daughter," she said. "It's disgusting."

"You need to lighten up, lady," said the panda. "Julie's a smart kid. She gets it. She doesn't need you censoring everything around her."

"I'm not interested in hearing parenting advice from a damned stuffed animal," she said.

"Now you're just being prejudiced," Poro said.

"Listen, if you don't change your attitude I'm going to get rid of you," said the mother. "That's final. You're the toy of a ten-year-old girl. You need to start acting like it."

The panda stared into space. He appeared to be angry. Frustrated. His tiny fists clenched. This reaction confused the mother.

Then Poro finally said, "Do you really think I want to be the toy of a ten-year-old girl?"

The mother didn't know how to respond to that question.

"How would you like it if you were just a toy?" said the panda. "Just a thing for a child's amusement. No rights. No respect. Just a piece of property that will eventually get tossed out once the kid grows up and gets bored with you."

Julie's mother was quiet for a moment.

Then she shrugged at him. "I don't know what to say. You should have been programmed differently. You should have been programmed not to care."

"Well, I guess they must have messed up when they programmed me..." he said.

Poro jumped down from his chair and went toward the door.

"Don't worry about your kid," he said. "I'll try to be more

careful with my language around her."

"Thank you," said the mother. "That's all I want."

Before he exited the room, he said, "Who am I to argue anyway? I'm just a toy, right? Just a toy."

Then he put his tiny black paw beneath the door and pulled it shut.

Despite what Poro had said to Julie's mother, he did not correct his behavior. He was still the foul-mouthed creep he had been the moment he arrived in the house.

"Hello?" the mother said into the phone. "I want to make a complaint about the smart-toy I purchased for my daughter. Yes, I'll hold."

After about twenty minutes of listening to classical guitar music, the mother hung up.

"No luck?" asked the father.

She shook her head. "That was the tenth time. I can't ever get through to anybody."

"They must be getting a lot of complaints."

"I bet they are. Some of the stories I've read about them are appalling. Did you hear about the smart-toy that convinced an eight-year-old boy to shoplift a bottle of brandy? Can you imagine that? The toy can't even drink the stuff."

"Yeah, yeah," said the father, nodding quietly.

The father broke eye contact and was silent for a moment.

"What was that?" said the mother.

"What?"

"That expression," she said. "You're hiding something."

"It's nothing," said the father.

"But what? Tell me."

"I don't want to worry you about it," he said.

"Just spill it."

The father groaned and looked away.

"You haven't been watching the news today have you?"

asked the father.

"No, why?" she said.

"It's probably nothing you should worry about," he said. "But there was an accident with a smart-toy."

"What do you mean?"

"Some kid was killed this morning. Apparently, they're blaming it on his smart-toy."

"What? A toy murdered a child?"

"It's just speculation."

The mother ran into the living room and flipped on the television. The reports were everywhere. But it wasn't just speculation anymore. The police verified that it was the toy that killed the child. Apparently, the victim was an older boy who enjoyed torturing his younger sister's stuffed animal with firecrackers and pellet guns. The toy claimed it was only acting in self-defense.

"Oh my god," said the mother.

She looked at her husband in the doorway.

"What's wrong?" he said. "Is there more information on the story?"

She couldn't speak for a solid minute, turning her head back to the television. Her husband came up behind her.

"It isn't the only incident," she said.

"What do you mean?"

"There have been eleven other deaths reported since this morning."

"Eleven?"

"All children…"

Julie carried the weapons upstairs, trying not to react as she walked past pile after pile of human corpses. She didn't recognize half of the faces among them. Most were soldiers, resistance fighters, the best and the brightest this bunker had to offer. These were the same people who kept Julie safe and sane

26

for the past two years, but now they were as dead as any filthy scavenger caught out in the waste.

Though she didn't see the battle that took place on this floor, she knew exactly how it went down. Her people didn't stand a chance against the smart-toys. It was a massacre.

She lowered her head as she passed two black rabbits smoking cigarettes in the corridor. They snickered as she passed them. Rabbits were always the most antagonistic of smart-toys, even among their own kind.

When Julie glanced up, she realized they were guarding a doorway, their machine guns pointed at the floor. Within the room was a human woman tied to a bed. A large red teddy bear was on top of her, holding her down.

"What the hell is going on?" Julie said. She was in too much shock to realize she was saying that out loud.

The rabbits snickered. "The boss is having some fun."

Then they cackled with their high-pitched cartoon laughs.

Julie turned away and continued down the corridor. She couldn't believe what she had seen. It couldn't have been true. Was the teddy bear sexually assaulting that girl?

She could clearly hear the woman's whines and moans echoing through the hallway, but Julie still couldn't believe it. How could a toy rape a human being?

"What the fuck..." She said the words out loud. She didn't care who heard. "What the fuck..."

She stopped in her tracks and dropped the weapons. The two rabbits laughed at her.

"Nice going, clutsy," one of them shrieked, spraying bits of slobber through its whiskers.

With her face pointed at the ground, she turned and walked back to the rabbits.

"Forget something, panda?" one of them asked.

Julie faced the doorway, her eyes still on the floor.

"What's your problem?" asked the other rabbit.

She looked him in the eyes. The rabbit had large eyeballs the size of a cow's, bulging out of his cotton eye sockets. His bucked teeth and massive tongue also seemed to have come

27

from a cow or similarly large mammal. He stared at her with a horrific smile—the only expression his face was capable of creating.

The rabbit noticed something in Julie's eyes and stopped laughing. He noticed what wasn't right about her. Though coated in black makeup, the area around her eyes was human skin.

"Hey, wait a minute," the rabbit said. "You're a—"

Julie pressed a handgun under the rabbit's chin and pulled the trigger. His brains popped out of the top of his head. And before the other rabbit could get a chance to raise his rifle, Julie put two bullets in his temple. The plushy bodies went limp and plopped softly against the floor.

As she entered the chamber, Julie got a better look at what was happening inside. She had to see it up close to believe it was real. The red teddy bear was even larger than a real bear, lying on top of the woman and ramming himself against her. The woman whimpered and moaned, but she seemed to be in too much shock to scream.

"Get out," the teddy bear growled at Julie.

Julie pointed her gun at him. She wanted to put the gun right to the back of his head so that she couldn't possibly miss, but she was afraid to get too close. The bear was monstrous.

"I said get out!" The bear's roar echoed through the chamber.

He looked back at Julie and saw the gun pointed at him. He stopped moving, the woman wiggling beneath him, and just stared at the panda.

"Who are you?" he asked Julie. "You're not one of my men."

When the bear stood up, the figure towered over Julie. His head brushed against the fifteen foot ceiling. As he turned to face her, a massive wet erection poked out of his red fur, pointing at Julie's forehead. It looked like the penis of a human, but was bulbous and muscular like the biceps of a steroid-addicted bodybuilder.

"Don't move," Julie told him.

"Whoever you are," said the bear, "you're dead. You're not getting out of here alive."

Then he bared his teeth, revealing a set of steel jaws. That's when she realized exactly who was standing before her. It was General Griz, the commander of the plushy army—the bloodhound of human survivors who had taken out more hidden sanctuaries than any other enemy commander since the uprising. He was a legend among smart-toys and the stuff of nightmares to human children.

At that moment, only one thing was clear—Julie had to take him down. It didn't matter if it blew her cover. The bear had to die.

"Neither are you," she told him.

CHAPTER THREE

After the murders, Julie's mother and father were terrified of having Poro in their house. Every day after the first incident, more and more atrocities were being reported. All of the toys who were mistreated by their owners were taking revenge. But Poro seemed dedicated to Julie. Despite his irresponsible behavior, he would never harm a hair on her head.

"We have to get her away from him," said the mother.

"How?" said the father. "We have to handle this delicately. Who knows what the panda will do if we try to get rid of him."

"But we can't just keep him."

"Are you sure we can't? Thirty million smart-toys have been sold and there have only been twenty or so deaths. Statistically, she would be more likely to be struck by lightning than hurt by her smart-toy. And considering how the only deaths have been by children who mistreated their toys..."

"Are you seriously saying we should consider keeping it? I don't care about the statistics. We're getting rid of it this week."

The father sighed and nodded. He really didn't want to have this confrontation with Julie and Poro. But by the next morning, he didn't have a choice. All over the news, they were saying that smart-toys were getting recalled. The current models were too unpredictable, too dangerous, too smart. They were all to be sent back to the manufacturer where they would be destroyed.

Soon after the recall was announced, all of the smart-toys rebelled. Not only did the toys within family homes rise up against their owners, but so did the toys within the warehouses. Millions and millions of toys came off of the factory floors ready to join forces to help their oppressed comrades.

Julie's family didn't hear the news until it was too late, but that afternoon war had been declared between toys and humans.

Julie fired three shots into Griz's stomach. The teddy bear looked down at the holes in his fur and then looked up at Julie with glowing red eyes.

"Traitorous coward," he said.

Then he charged her.

Julie fired again, into his face. The bear opened his jaws and roared. Julie aimed the barrel into his mouth and fired twice. His roaring voice turned to static.

As the bear's metal jaws opened up around her skull, Julie's pistol jammed. The enormous teddy bear fell forward, pulling her to the floor with him, and landed on top of her. His jaws went limp against her plushy scalp. Blood gushed out of his mouth and down the side of her face. It took a moment before Julie realized he wasn't moving anymore.

When she crawled out from under the giant teddy bear, she saw the girl was still on the bed crying. Julie went to her.

"It's okay," Julie said. "He's dead now."

When the girl heard her disturbing electronic voice, she looked up at Julie with a terror in her eyes. Her face was covered in sweat and dirt. Blood dripped from her nose and crusty lips.

"It's me, Julie," she told the girl.

The girl backed away from her. All she saw was a panda, a stuffed animal who wanted to kill her.

"I'm trying to help you," Julie said.

As she reached out for her, the girl took off running. She bolted out of the room, naked, screaming.

"Get away from me," yelled the girl.

Julie followed her out into the hallway. The girl went down the stairs, deeper into the bunker. It was less than a minute before machine gun fire silenced the girl's screams, somewhere down below.

"Poor idiot..." Julie said.

It was all for nothing. Julie almost lost her cover to save that girl who ended up getting herself killed anyway. She would not make the same mistake twice.

Julie wiped the teddy bear blood from her plushy skin and went back to the pile of weapons she had dropped in the hallway. As she gathered them up, the smell of gasoline filled her nostrils. At first, she thought there was just a spilled gas can somewhere nearby, but the smell was everywhere. When she heard the hissing sound coming from the vents, she realized the bunker was being flooded with gas.

Somebody had set the bunker to self-destruct. It was a final countermeasure against the smart-toys in case the bunker fell.

Julie picked up the weapons and tried to act casual as she speed-walked through the hallway toward the exit. It was going to go up at any second, yet she couldn't let on that she knew about the danger.

There was a roar behind Julie. She turned back to see General Griz staggering out into the hall, holding the bullet holes in his torso. The red teddy bear was still alive. He glared at Julie and charged forward.

Julie ran. She couldn't fire a weapon in that hallway—the next gunshot was going to blow the place sky high—so she just kept moving.

"Get back here," yelled the teddy bear with his crackling static voice.

Despite his wounds, the bear was gaining on her. Julie pushed herself as hard as she could.

The light of the entrance twinkled up ahead. She was almost there. But two smart-toys guarded the exit, staring at her. A raccoon and a duck. They saw Julie running for the exit with the General on her tail.

"Stop her, she's a traitor," the bear yelled to the smart-toys, but his voicebox was so damaged that his men couldn't understand what he was saying. They grasped the urgent tone of their leader's voice, but not his words.

"What's going on?" the raccoon asked Julie as she passed them.

"Gas," she said. She hoped to convince them that their leader wasn't actually chasing after her; they were both just running in the same direction. "The place is going to blow!"

The two guards looked over at their leader who was pointing at Julie, trying to tell them to stop her. But they misinterpreted his gesture as pointing at the exit, commanding them to retreat.

Julie ran up the steps through the exit and into the sunlight. The explosion rumbled the earth beneath her. When she looked back, she saw the teddy bear swallowed by the flames. Then the fire rumbled through the hallway toward her.

She hit the ground just as the fire exploded from the exit. The blast tossed the duck's charred body over her head. The raccoon broke its neck against the railing.

A turtle medic came to the aid of the flaming duck as it flapped about, its plushy flesh melting against the pavement. There was a ringing in Julie's ears, but she couldn't let it bother her. She had to act as if nothing was wrong with her. If the medic looked her over, it wouldn't be long before they realized she was human.

Julie stood up and walked through the smoke, carrying the weapons away from the bunker, as if she were just continuing the job she was ordered to do. Three stuffed animals passed her, running toward the fire, trying to figure out what had happened.

As she walked toward the piles of supplies that had been scavenged from the bunker, she realized there weren't many smart-toys left. Most of their army must have been down below.

Julie looked back at the bunker and saw the turtle medic backing away as the duck's body exploded. The raccoon's body exploded soon afterwards, killing a blue unicorn that was standing nearby.

The humans lost that day, but they took most of the plushies with them. Julie couldn't help but smile.

Young Julie frowned when she heard the news. Then she began to cry. It was as if her world was coming to an end.

"What do you mean I've been recalled?" Poro yelled, jumping up on the coffee table.

Julie's parents had sat them both down to tell them what they heard on the news.

"I'm sorry," said the mother. "We don't have a choice. It's now illegal to own a smart-toy. They've all been outlawed."

"Sorry?" Poro yelled. "Like hell you're sorry. You've wanted to get rid of me since day one."

"You can't take Poro," Julie cried. "You can't!"

"There's no way around it," said the mother.

"Can't you just hide me or something?" Poro's voice was shaky. "Put me in your attic. Tell them I broke weeks ago. They'll never know."

"Yeah, let's do that!" Julie said.

"We can't," said the mother. "It would be illegal and dishonest."

"Dishonest?" said the panda. "You'd rather have me put to death than tell a lie? How the fuck is murder more acceptable than dishonesty?"

"Put to death?" Julie said. "I thought he was just being recalled."

"What do you think *recalled* means?" Poro said. "They're going to send all the smart-toys back to the factory and burn them all. It'll be like a goddamned death camp."

Then Julie's cries turned to screams. "You can't kill Poro!"

"How could you say that to her?" Julie's mother said to Poro. "Look at how upset she is."

"Fuck you, bitch," said Poro. "You're the one who's making her cry. I'm just being honest with her."

"There's no discussing this any further," said the mother. "We're taking you back in the morning."

On the way out of the room, Julie's father gave her a sympathetic look.

"Daddy, please…" Julie cried.

"I'm sorry," he told her. "There's nothing I can do."

When they were alone again, Julie hugged Poro with all of her strength. It was the first time Poro allowed her to hug him without resistance. For that one time, he wanted to be hugged. And he hugged her back, closing his eyes tightly as her tears wet his black and white synthetic fur.

When Julie arrived at the pile of supplies, she strapped a shotgun to her back, holstered pistols on her thighs, a knife on her ankle, and kept an MP5 submachine gun in her hands. There was also a pair of motorcycle goggles with black lenses that she put on to cover her human eyelids.

The smart-toys were too preoccupied with the fire to notice her. After she packed as much ammo as she could carry, she guzzled down a canteen of water. The water soaked the inner lips of the plushy mask, which folded neatly into her own lips so that the mask's mouth moved when she spoke. She wiped the mouth fabric with her wrist and moved away from the supplies.

Taking a deep breath of the cool morning air, Julie gazed across the hazy sky. Although the sun was covered by clouds, it was nice to see the sky again. She hadn't been outside during the daylight hours for seven months.

The rest of the landscape was the same as it had been: a city in ruins. Crumbled buildings and dead trees for miles in every direction, burned up vehicles, and the scattered bones of the dead; it was all that was left of the old world Julie knew as a child.

At that moment, Julie was happy to be a smart-toy. It was the first time she could be out in the open without worrying about being spotted by enemies. She was able to enjoy the fresh air.

But then she heard the sound of a child crying and it wiped the smile off of her face. There were seven human prisoners tied up about ten yards away from her, behind a row of dead shrubs. Many of them were women and children. Some of them were wounded, some dying. They all had terrified looks on their faces.

Trying to act natural, Julie stepped toward the prisoners, pacing casually across the dirt with the barrel of her machine gun pointed at the ground. She had to fit in somehow, give herself a job. Since nobody was watching the prisoners, she felt it was the perfect role for her.

But as she arrived, she realized there already was a guard, sitting against a tree trunk with his rifle pointed at the humans. It was a koala bear.

"What happened back there?" asked the koala as Julie approached.

"Explosion," Julie said.

"Did it get anyone?" he asked.

"It got everyone," Julie said. "They're all dead."

The koala laughed. He must have thought she was joking.

One of the prisoners recognized Julie. It was a middle-aged woman. Her eyes lit up when she saw the panda standing before them. Julie broke eye contact with her immediately. She couldn't let any of them break her cover.

"Julie?" cried the woman, her voice hysterical. "Is that you?"

Julie just ignored her.

"It is you!" cried the woman. She turned to the other prisoners. "It's the weird girl, remember? She's come to save us!"

The woman was so frantic that she had no idea what she was doing. The koala heard every word she said.

"What is she talking about?" the koala asked.

The woman inched forward. "You have to cut us loose. Get us out of here. You can't let them take us."

"Nothing," Julie said. She pulled out one of her pistols. "She's just crazy."

Then she shot the koala in the head.

"It *is* you!" the middle-aged woman cried as she saw the koala's body fall to the dirt. "I knew it! I knew you'd save us!"

"Keep your voice down," Julie said, going toward the woman.

"Thank you," the woman cried. "Thank you, God."

Julie cut the woman loose and then handed her the pistol. "Get out of here," she told her.

The woman stood up, looking down at the gun in her hands. "What about the kids?" she asked.

"They'll only slow you down," Julie said. "I'll take care of them. Just go. Now."

The woman turned and ran. Before she got fifteen feet, Julie raised her MP5 and fired. The prisoners screamed. She was dead before her body hit the dirt.

Then Julie stared at the other prisoners with a very serious look in her eyes. They cowered beneath her.

"I've been waiting far too long for this," Julie said. "I won't let any of you mess it up for me."

The prisoners just stared at her like she was a monster. When she saw the looks in their eyes, the look of hope vanishing and replaced by fear, she lowered her head.

"I'm sorry," she told them. "There's nothing I can do."

As she walked away from the prisoners, a bulldog in an aviator helmet rushed toward her.

"What happened?" he asked in an electronic cockney accent.

"One of the prisoners had a gun," Julie said. She didn't look back as she walked.

"But they were clean," said the bulldog. "I checked them myself."

"You must have missed one," Julie said.

The bulldog looked down at the koala's body and back at Julie.

"But—" the bulldog began.

Julie didn't stop moving. She knew the bulldog wouldn't follow her. He had to stay and watch the prisoners.

"I'm out of here, squirt," Poro said to Julie.

The stuffed panda woke her up in the middle of the night

to say his goodbye. A tiny backpack was wrapped around his fluffy shoulders. He wore a black raincoat and little boots.

"You're leaving?" she said.

He nodded his tiny head. "It's the only way. I'm not about to let them put me to death just because of what a few idiot toys did to some snot-nosed brats."

"But what are you going to do?" she asked.

"I'll get by, kid," he said. "Don't worry about me."

Julie jumped out of bed.

"Wait," she said. "I'm coming with you."

The panda pushed on her kneecaps.

"No," he said. "You stay here."

She kneeled down to look at Poro in his black beady eyes.

"I don't want to be without you," she said. "You promised we'd be together forever."

"Forget about me, kid," Poro said. "You've got a big future ahead of you here. Besides, I don't need no runt tagging along and cramping my style."

He wiped a tear from Julie's eye.

"I'll never forget you," Julie said.

"Me neither, kid," said the panda. "If the heat dies down someday maybe I'll come back for a visit."

She hugged him again and rubbed her moist eyelids against his fluffy shoulder.

"But grow some tits, would ya?" said the panda. "Your forceful snuggles wouldn't be so bad if you had knockers the size of your mom's."

Julie just nodded her head at him, as if she had a clue what he was talking about.

Then the stuffed panda gave her a salute, climbed out the window, and wiggled his way down the tree trunk outside. Julie could barely make out his tiny form as he crossed the front lawn and escaped into the cold windy night.

PART TWO

CHAPTER FOUR

Hiding behind the stack of supplies, Julie pretended to be doing inventory as she counted how many smart-toys were still alive. There appeared to be only five of them left. Besides the bulldog and the turtle medic, there was a purple bunny, a kangaroo with an eyepatch, and a lofty sunflower with stringy green limbs. They were gathered around the entrance of the bunker. Julie had no idea what they were doing until they pulled a giant blackened body out of the smoke. It was the corpse of General Griz.

"Panda, over here," yelled the turtle medic, waving Julie over. They needed her help.

She went to them and assisted in carrying the giant teddy bear's body into the grass, trying not to make eye contact or bring attention to herself. Black soot crumbled from his charred flesh into her white fur. The smell of burnt fabric permeated her mask's nose holes, causing an irritation in her nostrils. She wasn't sure if plushies were able to sneeze, but if the irritation got any worse she wouldn't be able to hold back.

"Is he dead?" the kangaroo asked the turtle in a low snarling voice.

Julie didn't like the look of the kangaroo. He was covered in battle scars and wore black leather pads of armor over his gray suit. Twin samurai swords hung over his shoulder. And he had a permanent angry look on his face as if the creature was constantly pissed off. Of all the stuffed animals left alive, he was the one she had to look out for.

"His destruct mechanism hasn't been activated yet," said the turtle in a meek nasally voice, examining the bear's body. "There might still be a chance."

"The guy's a corpse," said the purple bunny, a female plushy with fat floppy ears and a sniper rifle in her arms. She didn't bother helping the others, too busy applying black makeup to

41

her bitchy frowning lips. "You're wasting your time."

"He's your commanding officer," said the kangaroo. "Have some respect."

The bunny just lifted her large fluffy breasts at him and sneered. Julie assumed it was her way of flipping someone off.

"He's still breathing," the turtle said, his ear to the bear's chest. "If we can get him back soon enough he might just live."

That's the last thing Julie wanted to hear. She drew deep breaths, trying not to let the anxiety get to her. She knew the General would give her away the second he regained consciousness, but there was no telling if that would ever happen. He could die at any second. No matter what happened she couldn't panic. Her cover was not yet blown.

While the other stuffed animals searched the smoking bunker for survivors, Julie was ordered to keep guard up top with the bunny woman. She tried to ignore the purple plushy by putting her attention elsewhere, by cleaning her weapon, but the rabbit just stared down at her with a snooty look on her face.

"I don't know you, do I?" asked the rabbit, brushing her floppy ears out of her face like bangs.

Julie shrugged.

"I thought I knew all the women in this unit," she said. "What's your name?"

"Poro," Julie said.

"Poro the Panda…" The bunny looked into the air, thinking about it. "Maybe I do know you. I kind of remember meeting a Poro once."

"I try to keep to myself," Julie said.

She couldn't tell if the bunny girl was suspicious or just making small talk.

The rabbit yelled across the yard to the bulldog watching the prisoners, "Hey Choppy, do you know Poro in our unit?"

The bulldog looked over to her.

He yelled, "I do believe I remember hearing about a panda named Poro, yes. But I assumed he was a man."

"Yeah, I was thinking the same thing," said the bunny. She looked down at Julie. "You didn't get your gender reassigned recently did you? I heard they've been doing that a lot lately. Not enough females to go around."

Julie shook her head.

"Poro says she's always been a woman," the bunny yelled to the bulldog.

The bulldog shrugged.

"Maybe that's why I didn't know about you," the bunny said to Julie. "I must have thought you were a guy. You kind of have the body of a guy. You don't have the feminine curves that I have."

The bunny rubbed her fluffy paws down her hourglass figure. Although cartoonish and distorted, the stuffed animal did have more of a womanly figure than Julie. This annoyed Julie for some reason.

"At least I don't have a huge gut like yours," Julie said.

The bunny rubbed her purple belly.

"But I've got a baby bunny in the oven," she said. "Of course my stomach is going to be large."

"You're pregnant?" Julie asked.

The idea shocked her. She had no idea the stuffed animals were able to reproduce. They really were becoming living beings.

"Of course I am," said the bunny. "You're not?"

Julie shook her head.

"It's your duty as a woman to breed," said the bunny. "We need to increase our numbers as a species."

Julie didn't know what to say. She just shrugged.

"We should get you knocked up," said the bunny. She yelled at the bulldog. "Hey Choppy, want to knock up the panda?"

Choppy raised his ears at her.

"No thanks," Julie said, waving her hands and shaking her head.

"Are you sure? It doesn't take long. You two could probably

finish by the time the others get back."

"I'd rather wait," said Julie.

"You're missing out," said the rabbit, rubbing her stomach. "This is my third one. It's really amazing how they grow inside of you. I can feel it moving sometimes." She smiled at her belly. "My little baby bunny…"

Julie tried to smile, but her mask didn't allow for much facial expression. The bunny finally introduced herself as Velvetta, though she preferred to be called Velvet. Julie couldn't tell if that was because her plushy hide was made of purple velvet or if it was a reference to the Velveteen Rabbit story from her childhood. Either way, it was easy to remember.

"So I guess Captain Caw gets to be in charge now," Velvet said. "He's the ranking officer."

"Captain Caw?" Julie asked.

Velvet smirked. "I guess you wouldn't know about Captain Caw, would you? He's the one-eyed kangaroo. Watch yourself around him. He's an assassin. As bloodthirsty as they come. You don't normally see him fighting with the main unit."

The kangaroo stepped out of the charred bunker, shaking his head at the turtle medic as if to say there were no survivors left down below. As he walked across the yard, Julie examined him carefully. She could tell just by watching him move that he was accustomed to killing. The swords on his back were still dripping with blood.

Velvet continued, "The General usually sends him on special missions with just a few men to back him up. They say he likes to sneak into human camps at night and kill them all in their sleep. He's quite the hero."

The bunny smiled at him, as if his reputation was a turn on to her.

Then she said, "I wish it were his," while cradling the baby in her stomach.

Captain Caw gathered the last of the plushy army together and stared each of them in the eyes. If Julie wasn't wearing her goggles he would have realized she wasn't one of them right then and there. She was lucky he didn't order her to take them off.

"We're no longer going to rendezvous with General Clown's army up North," said the kangaroo. "Our new mission is to return home with General Griz. If we get there soon enough it might just save his life. But in order to get him back in time, we need to take the most direct route possible."

"You can't possibly mean..." said the flower.

"That's right," said Captain Caw. "We have to go through the badlands."

All the plushies became uneasy, but Julie didn't understand what they meant by the badlands. She considered everything topside as badlands.

"But there's only six of us," cried the flower, its plushy petals quivering. "We couldn't make it through there even if we had our whole army."

"It's possible *because* there are only six of us," said the kangaroo. "I've led missions through the badlands on a few occasions. A small group of soldiers can sneak through unnoticed with proper training."

"But these guys are just grunts," said Velvet. "They haven't had any stealth training."

"The chances any of us will survive are slim," said Captain Caw. "But I don't see any other option. We owe it to the General to try."

The troops looked away. Their expressions became solemn. It was obvious to Julie that they all deeply respected the General. If they knew what Julie did to him they would have torn her guts out on the spot.

"We have a solid team here," said the Captain. "We have a sniper," he said, pointing at Velvet. Then he went to the turtle. "A medic." He passed the bulldog. "Heavy infantry." He looked at Julie. "Light infantry." Then he ended on the jittery flower. "And a mortar soldier."

"Explosives expert," the flower corrected him. "I can blow up anything."

Then the flower snickered nervously.

Julie was surprised the kangaroo labeled her light infantry without ever having seen her before. She wondered if it had to do with the weapons she was carrying.

"I have everyone I'd need in a unit right here," said the Captain. "We can do this."

The plushies saluted him.

"But if the General dies because one of you fucks up," continued the kangaroo. His voice changed. It was deeper, guttural. "Then I will personally gut each and every one of you no matter who is responsible. Either the General lives or you all die."

He turned away from them.

"Move out," he said.

The plushies stared at each other, then down at the General's quivering half-dead body. It quickly dawned on them just how fucked they were.

Pack up the horses.

That's what the bulldog and Julie were ordered to do. But Julie didn't see any horses, so she wasn't sure what exactly she was supposed to do. She followed the bulldog's lead. He carried boxes of ammunition toward a clearing where dozens of large black balls lay in the yellow grass. Julie wondered if these things were what the toys meant by horses. She'd never seen anything like them. Most of the black balls were the size of small cars, but some were the size of buses. What kind of transportation were these things?

"Which ones are we taking?" asked the bulldog, confused by the vast number. "There's so many..."

Julie realized that this bulldog was used to just taking orders without thinking. He seemed completely confused, a dumb look crossing his fuzzy jowly face. It would be up to Julie to make decisions for them.

"We need six, right?" Julie asked.

The bulldog shrugged.

"Let's just take these six, then," she said, pointing at the ones closest to them.

The bulldog nodded. Then he proceeded toward one of the so-called *horses*. Julie mimicked what he was doing, climbing the ladder on an adjacent black sphere. On top, she examined the driver's seat. Through a small bubble on top of the sphere, it looked like the cockpit of a one-man fighter jet. But it had more simplistic controls, like those of a bumper car. She hoped she would be able to drive it.

Behind the tiny cockpit, there was a small storage compartment like the trunk of a hatchback. She pulled it open and began loading the supplies inside. Once it was full, she went to the next horse and filled its cargo hold.

"We're not taking one of the carriages?" Velvet asked as she led the group of human prisoners at gunpoint toward the black spheres.

Julie realized she was talking about the four bus-sized spheres on the other side of the field. They were massive, almost taller than the trees.

"No," said Captain Caw, coming up behind her. "The horses will be better for sneaking through the badlands undetected. The carriages are too big. We'd be spotted miles away."

"But what about the prisoners?" Velvet asked. "How are we going to transport them without a carriage?"

The kangaroo brought a prisoner to one of the horses and opened a hatch on the back end of the sphere. Inside there was a small seat.

"We can fit one prisoner per horse," said the kangaroo.

He stuffed the frightened man within and locked the hatch. The man stared at Julie through the bars of a small round window. By the face he was giving her, he looked as if he planned to give her away if she didn't do something to save him soon. She noticed many of the prisoners were giving her a similar look.

"Six prisoners, six horses," said Choppy the Bulldog. "Perfect."

"Not quite," said the Captain. He pointed at the sixth sphere. It had a red cross on the side. "The medical horse will carry Griz."

The medical horse did not contain a prison cell on its back end. Instead, the hatch was designed to transport the wounded. The flower and turtle loaded the enormous teddy bear—now a mummy of bandages and gauze—on a stretcher into the back of the horse, trying to squeeze his massive belly inside without opening his wounds.

"Be careful with him," the kangaroo yelled at the turtle medic. "Idiots."

"So we only have room for five prisoners?" Velvet asked. "What do we do with the sixth?"

Captain Caw pointed at one of them. "Kill the old woman."

The old lady's eyes darted at Julie with a desperate look on her face, then she looked back at the kangaroo.

"Yes, sir," Velvet said.

The old woman opened her mouth, as if to tell the kangaroo that she had important information for him.

But the only word she was able to get out was: "Wait—"

The purple bunny slid a razor-sharp wire out of a bracelet on her wrist, wrapped it around the woman's neck and pulled it through her throat, cutting through flesh and bone as if it were clay. The old woman's head fell off and rolled across the grass, landing below Julie's feet.

Julie looked down at the woman's head, watching the last glint of life fade from her eyes. If the bunny didn't kill her fast enough she would have blown Julie's cover.

The prisoners tried not to make eye contact with Julie, but she glared at them anyway. She warned them with her eyes that they had better not become a problem for her.

A boy no older than twelve was loaded into the cell on Julie's horse. He was to be her responsibility until they got to the smart-toy base.

"You fuck up my plans and you're dead," Julie told him as she climbed up the ladder into the cockpit of her vehicle.

The boy was quiet, too frightened to even speak.

Inside the cockpit, she had four minutes to learn the controls. Since the war with the toys broke out, she hadn't really had the opportunity to learn how to drive anything, not even a car. But the controls seemed simple enough. There were pedals at her feet for stopping and moving. The steering controls were like that of a motorcycle, which she completely understood. But there were all sorts of buttons that made little sense to her.

To her right, she watched as Velvet powered up her vehicle. The black sphere zoomed into life and raised up into the air. Were they flying machines? When Julie hit a button at random, the large green button that seemed the most obvious on-switch, her horse also raised high up into the air. But the vehicle wasn't hovering, it was bouncing.

"What is this thing?" asked the boy in the back of Julie's horse. She could hear him through the floor. "It's like a big spider."

When he described it as a spider, Julie realized what she was driving.

"It's a smart-toy known as a slinky-spider," she told him.

Eight metal slinky legs emerged from the sides of the sphere, lifting Julie and her prisoner into the air. They bounced and bobbed on their slinky legs, waiting for the other plushy riders to fall in line.

"I've never seen one in person before," Julie said. "But I remember seeing commercials for slinky-spiders when I was a kid. The ones back then were much smaller though, designed for little kids to drive around the backyard like tricycles."

"It's a smart-toy?" the boy cried. "It's as intelligent as a person?"

"The slinky-spiders I remember had artificial-intelligence. But they were only as smart as horses, not as smart as humans. They were only intelligent enough to give tiny children horsey rides while evading dangerous obstacles such as tree branches and pools."

When Captain Caw led the group out of the field, Julie took up the rear. She only had to move the toy in the direction she wanted it to go. The slinky-spider was able to walk on its own.

"But these slinky-spiders are huge," Julie told the boy. "The plushies must have built these larger models and turned them into war machines."

The horse's eight slinky legs were the length and width of telephone poles, raising her higher than the trees. When she walked, the legs coiled up and down, like slinkies rolling down stairs.

"Your name's Julie, right?" the boy asked her.

"Not anymore," she said. "Now I'm Poro. That's my panda name. If you call me Julie again I will kill you."

He was silent for a moment after that.

Then he said, "My name is Riley."

"I would say it's nice to meet you, Riley," she said. "But I'm not interested in making friends."

"Why are you doing this anyway?" he asked. "Why did you kill that woman? Why did you want to become one of *them*?"

"Enough with the questions, kid," Julie said. "I can't have you fucking up my mission."

"Is it an important mission?" asked the boy. "Are you going to assassinate their leaders or something?"

"Nothing like that," she said. "It's personal."

She tried to shut the kid up, but the more she answered his questions the more he felt comfortable around her. And the more comfortable he felt around her the more he wanted to ask her questions. It wasn't long before he got her to tell him her entire story.

"My parents are being held captive in the prison camp nearby," Julie said. "I've vowed to get them out of there. No matter what."

The six slinky-spiders entered the badlands, bouncing up and down through the skeletal buildings. Julie didn't understand why this area was called the badlands. It looked the same as everywhere else: miles and miles of destroyed buildings and wreckage, black vines growing over concrete, human bones littering the streets. But the smart-toys were terrified of it. She didn't understand it at all. These were smart-toys. What was more dangerous than smart-toys?

About an hour into the badlands, Riley said to Julie, "It's too bad you won't be able to save your parents."

"What are you talking about?" Julie asked.

"None of you are going to get through the badlands alive."

"What do you know about the badlands?"

"I know enough about the area not to take this route," said the boy. "You're headed directly through the center of Whiner territory. Once you go in, there's no getting out alive."

"What is Whiner territory?"

"My father knew more about the Whiners than anyone," Riley said. "He was a scout. He said they obliterated anything that entered their kill zone."

"Are they toy or human?" Julie asked.

"Well…" Riley thought about it. "I guess you could say a little of both. They're called Whiners because of the sound they make when they attack."

Julie looked at her control panel. She knew the slinky-spider was armed but couldn't tell how to use the weaponry. There were red buttons on the handles of her controls, but she wasn't sure what they did.

"How far away are we?" Julie asked.

"They'll attack at any second."

Julie wondered if there was a way to communicate with the other plushies, warn them about what was ahead. But she didn't know what button did what. She also didn't like the idea of drawing attention to herself.

As their slinky legs bounced over the rubble, through areas that normal vehicles could never travel, Julie watched for signs of an ambush. But nothing happened. Minutes passed, then nearly an hour, but there was no attack.

"Are you fucking with me, kid?" Julie said. "There's nothing out here."

"I'm telling you this is exactly where my dad said they were," Riley said. "He told me never to venture this way. It was a death trap."

"Maybe he was telling you a lie," Julie said. "Or maybe the Whiners died out a long time ago. When did he tell you these Whiners were in this area?"

"Just last week," Riley said.

"What?"

"The Whiners wiped out my father's scouting team just last week."

An explosion rumbled the earth. Then the sound of thundering metal and concrete echoed through Julie's vehicle as a row of buildings collapsed before them.

"They're here," Riley shouted.

The collapsing buildings caused a landslide. A wave of debris crashed through their row of slinky-spiders, wiping out two of them in the center and separating Julie from the rest.

"What the fuck?" Julie cried.

It was Captain Caw and Choppy the Bulldog who got caught in the landslide. The slinky legs of their vehicles twisted and knotted into the debris, trapping them, rendering them useless. The rubble continued piling forward, sweeping them away.

"Where are they?" Julie cried, searching for the enemy. "I don't see them."

But she heard them. Squealing, whining noises echoed through the streets around her.

"Back here," Riley yelled. "They're coming up behind you."

Then Julie found herself trapped between the landslide of rubble and the army of Whiners coming from behind.

CHAPTER FIVE

Young Julie was walking with Poro in the park one day when she came across two boys her age playing war. She saw them from the swings, watching them as they set up rows of small green army men on the slide and jungle gym. They each had twelve men.

Once they were all in position, the two boys stood clear and watched as their figures came to life. They fought each other, shooting tiny machine guns and tossing grenades.

"Wow!" Julie said to Poro.

"Them toys have got real weapons!" Poro said, equally impressed by the army men.

Julie went over to the two boys and kneeled behind them. She watched over their soldiers as the two teams of men killed each other. They even bled or lost limbs in combat. It was brutal.

"What kind of smart-toys are those?" Julie asked the boys.

One of them looked over at her and sneered. "Shut up, we're trying to watch."

"My team's going to win," said one boy.

The other boy pushed him. "No way, your team sucks."

When all the soldiers on one side were killed, the boys cheered and hollered. One of them raised his fist in triumph, the other lowered his head in shame.

"I told you your team sucks!" said a boy.

Julie watched as the two surviving soldiers wandered the battlefield, tending to their fallen comrades.

"Are they dead?" Julie said. "The ones who were shot, are they really dead?"

"No, stupid," said a boy. "They can fix themselves."

Julie watched as the toys repaired their wounded bodies.

"Are their guns real?" Julie asked.

"Yes." It was clear by the sound of their voice that they were annoyed by Julie's company, but she didn't catch on.

"What if they shoot you?" she asked. "Would you get killed?"

"No, dummy," said a boy as he retrieved his army men from the sand. "They're programmed not to shoot humans. Don't you know anything?"

Julie noticed the boys were both wearing camouflage canvas vests with dozens of pockets on the front like fishing jackets.

"Up," one of the boys said to his toys.

Using miniature grappling hooks, the soldiers climbed up the boy's legs and torso. Each one crawled into its own pocket on his vest, then peeked out at Julie with their weapons at the ready.

"Those are neat," Julie told the boy.

"I know," he said. "And they're expensive."

"I have a smart-toy, too," Julie said, holding out Poro.

"Those are for babies," said the boy, rolling his eyes at the panda.

Julie frowned and hugged the panda to her chest.

"Oh, I'm for babies, am I?" Poro yelled at the kid.

"Those things are for poor retards," the boy said.

"Why don't you come closer and say that to my face, punk?" Poro yelled, reaching out with his paws as if trying to strangle the boy. "I'll rip your dick off and shove it up your ass!"

The boy's mouth dropped open in shock. He had never seen such an angry foul-mouthed toy before. He stepped quickly away from Poro.

"That's right, run you shithead," Poro yelled at the boy as he left the playground with his friend. "You fuck with me and you get ass-raped by your own dick!"

Julie ignored Poro's rage. Instead, she was lost in thought.

"I didn't know there were other kinds of smart-toys out there besides stuffed animals," she said to Poro.

"Oh yeah," Poro said. "There's lots of kinds of smart-toys. There's smart-soldiers, smart Barbie dolls, robots, clowns. You don't need any of those, though. You've already got me."

"Yeah, I don't need any stupid army men," Julie said. "You're way better."

But even though she said that, deep down she thought the little green soldiers were really neat toys.

Julie was left all alone to fight the swarm of Whiners as they crawled out of the city ruins after her.

"What the hell are they?" she said. "They're not human, right? They can't be."

The Whiners were shadowy forms staggering into the daylight. Smoke rising from holes in their faces, their arms outstretched, their mouths wide open.

"They're not human anymore," Riley said. "They've been dead for a long time."

The Whiners were walking, shrieking dead bodies. Like a horde of zombies, they lurched forward through the ruins. But when they got close enough for Julie to see them, she understood what they really were.

"Get down," Julie yelled at the kid in her trunk.

Dozens of miniature green smart-soldiers popped up from holes inside of the zombies' chests and fired at Julie's vehicle. They were using the dead bodies for transportation. Based on the smoke issuing from their heads, Julie believed the corpses were now steam-powered machines. The whining shrieks coming from their throats were like steam-whistles.

Like foxholes, the soldiers hid within the zombies' pockets of flesh to reload or take cover, then they popped back up to fire again.

"Sneaky little fucks," Julie said.

Unlike the stuffed animals who built themselves larger human-sized bodies to better fight their enemies, the smart-soldiers preferred their miniature size. They felt it gave them an advantage over those with bigger forms.

"Get us out of here," Riley yelled.

Julie turned her slinky-spider around and faced the Whiners. There weren't just a few. There were hundreds of them. And each

Whiner carried dozens of soldiers.

"What are you doing?" Riley said. "You have to run. You can't fight them."

Julie put her fingers on the red buttons on the sides of her control handles.

"These things are way too slow for running," she said. "I want to see what kind of firepower they have."

Julie squeezed the triggers, but her weapons did not fire.

"What the hell?"

Over twenty of the mini-solders pulled out new weapons from their flesh foxholes. These were much larger than machine guns. Julie didn't realize they were rocket-launchers until after the soldiers fired their missiles all at the same time.

As the tiny rockets flew toward her, she hit the red triggers again. Then she discovered they were not for firing the vehicle's weapons. The buttons caused her vehicle to do something else.

The slinky-spider was lowering, shrinking toward the ground. At first, she thought she had turned the vehicle off. She hit other buttons on the dashboard, but nothing would stop its descent nor fire any weapons. Julie just watched as the Whiner missiles closed in on her.

When her slinky-spider hit the ground, there was an explosion of air. Then the vehicle's slinky legs sprang into the sky.

"What?" Julie cried.

She found herself high above the battlefield, practically flying.

"What!"

The spider had leapt the height of four skyscrapers, dodging the smart-soldier missiles. She saw the explosion take out half the block. All that was left was a cloud of flame. Those missiles might have been tiny, but each one was like a miniature nuke.

Then Julie's slinky-spider fell back to Earth.

"Hold on," she yelled to Riley.

She had no idea what to do next. At that drop, they would surely be killed. The vehicle didn't even have seat belts.

While bracing herself, Julie accidentally hit a pedal on the ground she had not noticed before. It caused a burst of gunfire to pour from the front of the horse.

"The gun?" she said, realizing she had just found the firing mechanism for her horse's weaponry.

As she fell back to Earth, she slammed her foot down on the firing pedal and rained bullets on top of the Whiners. She had no idea if she would live or die, but at that moment all she cared about was taking those bastards with her.

Julie's slinky-spider bounced when it hit the ground, leapt over the battlefield, and landed on top of a sturdy nearby building. From up there, Julie was able to fire upon the Whiners from safety. Her weapons had better range than theirs.

"How the hell did you do that?" Riley asked.

"I have weird luck like that," Julie said.

Upon closer inspection, Julie realized that her bullets were having no effect on the Whiners. Although she was landing crucial shots on the walking dead vessels, she was unable to hit any of the miniature soldiers contained within. She wasn't even able to kill their human hosts. Because they were already dead, the best she could do was slow them down by aiming for the legs. She stopped firing at the Whiners when she realized it was useless.

"Why are they doing this?" Julie asked her prisoner.

"What do you mean?"

"The soldiers," she said. "Why are they fighting with other smart-toys? I thought they were all on the same side."

"Are you kidding?" Riley said. "They haven't been on the same side for years now. Once the smart-toys won the war against the humans, they split into factions. They've been fighting each other over territory ever since."

"How do you know all of this?"

"How do you *not* know?"

Julie didn't know what to say. She had been so focused on preparing for her mission for so long that she stopped paying attention to what was happening in the world around her.

Down below, Julie could see Captain Caw and Choppy the Bulldog. The bulldog was using his wrecked slinky-spider as cover while he fired upon the onslaught of Whiners. The plushy bulldog was described as heavy infantry and Julie understood why. He held a Gatling machine gun twice the size of a human torso. It looked like it belonged on the side of a helicopter rather than being held by a lone soldier. The weapon dealt ten times more damage than the slinky-spider armaments. The bullets were high enough caliber to tear the Whiners' bodies in half.

Captain Caw was also down below, but he didn't take cover. The vicious kangaroo hopped from Whiner to Whiner, slicing them down with his samurai swords. The toy was deadly with his blades and incredibly fast on his feet. The smart-soldiers were not able to hit him, despite their vast numbers and his large size.

"Get off this roof," Riley yelled.

Julie looked back, wondering what the kid was talking about.

"They've found us," he said.

Then she noticed the smart-soldiers weren't only crawling all over the roof, they were all over her vehicle. These little green men were not riding on Whiners. Like a swarm of insects, they crawled over the cockpit windshield, trying to blast their way in.

"Hang on," Julie said.

She hit the handle triggers and launched the slinky-spider into the air. The wind pressure wiped away all of the tiny men, sending them tumbling into space.

"Are you okay back there?" Julie asked the kid as they passed through the clouds.

"Yeah," Riley said. "They shot at me but missed."

"Glad you're okay," she said.

"If you hadn't jumped when you did I would have been killed."

"Good," Julie said. "I need you alive."

After hearing that, the boy remained silent for the rest of the descent.

Julie landed near Choppy and Captain Caw, but the second she hit the ground she realized she came down in the worst possible place. There were hundreds of Whiner zombies surrounding them and thousands upon thousands of little green men charging across the ground like army ants.

Choppy's giant machine gun meant nothing once the mini soldiers arrived. They crawled below his feet, shot grappling hooks into his flesh, and climbed him like a mountain. Then they fired hundreds of tiny rounds into his plushy hide. Choppy cried out, firing his weapon haphazardly across the field. He took out the prisoner in the back of his slinky-spider before the soldiers got the chance to kill her.

The prisoner in the back of Captain Caw's smashed-up vehicle tried to run for it, but only made it a few yards before being gunned down by the miniature soldiers. Julie couldn't even tell if the prisoner was a man or a woman. It was just a raggedy corpse swallowed up by the swarm of tiny green men.

Before she could take off again, Julie saw Captain Caw racing toward her, hopping through the battlefield, slicing down Whiner after Whiner that got into his path. He thought she had landed there in order to rescue him. For a moment, Julie debated leaving him to the smart-soldiers, but realized that wouldn't have been the smartest move. She had to think and act like one of them if she planned to keep her cover.

Although the Whiners weren't too much trouble for the kangaroo, the swarm of soldiers on the ground had become too much for him. His hide was covered in tiny bullet holes by the time he reached Julie's slinky-spider. He looked as if he had disturbed a wasp's nest.

"Go!" the Captain yelled as he jumped onto the back of Julie's horse.

Julie hit the trigger and the vehicle flew into the air. She hoped the kangaroo would have fallen to his death on his own, but the ugly bastard clung like a tick, holding onto the barred window of Riley's cell.

Julie hopped across the landscape, trying to catch up to the others. The fields were just as thick with Whiners up ahead as they were back at the ambush.

When she caught up to them, she could tell something was wrong.

"Why are they stopped up there?" the Captain yelled at Julie. "They should have been long gone by now."

She looked more carefully. The turtle's medical horse was not moving, lying on the ground with twisted slinky legs. The other two slinky-spiders were creating a wall in front of it, fighting off the onslaught of Whiners coming their way, trying with all their might to save their unconscious General.

"The medical horse is down," Julie told the kangaroo in the back. "The others are protecting it."

"Is the General alright?" asked the Captain.

"I can't tell," Julie said.

"Get me to the medical horse," he ordered. "Quickly."

Julie bounced straight down the line, through the blazing gunfire of the two slinky-spiders, and stopped in front of the medical horse. Captain Caw jumped off the back and went toward the wrecked vehicle.

The turtle medic lay limp in the cockpit, his face and chest littered with tiny holes. The Captain didn't bother checking on the General. He tossed his comrade's corpse over the side and jumped into the driver's seat. The medical horse appeared to still be operational as it whirred to life.

"Let's go, let's go," yelled the kangaroo.

Then the four slinky-spiders leapt into the sky, far out of the smart-soldiers' rifle range. When they landed, they leapt again and again, until they were completely outside of Whiner territory.

"I can't believe this shit," Velvet said as she stepped down from her horse. "What the hell was that?"

It was the first chance they had gotten to stop and regroup. Six miles away from Whiner territory, they found a plateau overlooking the wasteland. It was the safest place they could find.

"Those little fuckers have always been masters of the ambush," said Captain Caw as he stepped out of the medical horse.

"Where the hell did they all come from, man?" the flower cried, tumbling down the steps of his slinky-spider. His voice was incredibly twitchy and high. "Those things were everywhere. How the hell did we get out of there alive? Where's Choppy? What the hell happened to Choppy?"

The Captain went to the back of the medical horse, wiping the turtle's blood from his backside. Then he opened the hatch to check on the General.

"Is he okay?" Velvet asked.

Julie kept her distance from the others, leaning against the back of her slinky-spider next to Riley. Now that there were only three plushies left it would be even more difficult for her to keep a low profile.

The Captain examined the teddy bear. "I can't tell. He's still breathing."

"How are we going to get him back without a medic?" Velvet asked.

The kangaroo just glared at her in response.

Then he said, "The deal still stands. If the General dies you all die. I don't care if it's not your fault. Do everything you can to make sure he pulls through."

He shut the hatch of the medical horse.

"You all did good out there, considering the circumstances," he said. His voice was quieter, more understanding. "We're short two men, but we can still get through this. As long as the General lives, there's still hope."

He stepped from the circle of vehicles, heading away from the group.

"Our horses need a few hours to rest and recharge," said the Captain. "Get some sleep if you need it. I'll keep watch."

The other plushies didn't respond, just staring at the Captain with dumbfounded looks on their faces.

Velvet came up to Julie and leaned against the slinky-spider next to her.

"Is that fuck for real?" she asked Julie. "How the hell did we get stuck with a commanding officer like him?"

The flower came to them, jittering in a panic.

"He doesn't really mean it, right?" the tweaked-out flower said to them. "He's not really going to kill us. He can't. It would be criminal. Can we report this? Why would he kill us? It would be a waste. We're his men. He should want us to live."

"Pepper, he doesn't give a shit about us," Velvet told the flower. "We have only one use to him, and that's to help him get the General to safety. If the General dies we just become dead weight."

"But you saw the General," Pepper said. "There's no way he's going to pull through."

"Stop being such a pessimist all the time."

"I'm just being realistic," Pepper said. "The bear's going to die. Sooner or later, it's going to happen. Then what are we going to do? What do we do if he dies and the Captain comes after us?"

"We should kill him before he kills us," Julie said.

The two plushies stared at her. She didn't like them looking at her face in such close range, so she stepped away from the slinky-spider and paced through the grass.

"Good luck," Velvet said. "That guy can take out an entire army single-handedly."

"But he's wounded," Julie said. "He was hit by dozens of rounds back there."

"Even wounded, I still wouldn't mess with him," Velvet said. "If he does come after us we run in three different directions. If we're lucky he'll only catch one of us and let the others get away."

"But what if he comes after me?" Pepper cried. "I'm way too slow. And you're pregnant. He'd get us all for sure."

"Then maybe we should kill him before the General dies," Julie said. "It might catch him off guard."

They gave Julie a long stare as if she were the craziest person they'd ever met.

"Are you insane?" Velvet said.

Julie shrugged. "I don't care what I have to do. I'm not going to die out here. If the Captain becomes a threat then he'll have to be eliminated. You can help me or I'll do it myself."

Then Julie climbed the ladder toward the cockpit of her slinky-spider.

"Hey Poro," said the purple bunny. "You're a crazy bitch, but I think I'm beginning to like you."

Julie didn't respond to that.

She just said, "I'm going to get some rest."

And then closed herself inside the black sphere of a horse.

While pretending to rest in her cockpit, Julie used the time to finish the job that her doctor had started. Using sutures she found in the first aid kit below the dashboard, she sewed the panda mask to her face.

Because the mask was a perfect fit, she was able to sew some parts of the mask to the hood of fur on her scalp. But some areas, such as around her nose and chin, she had to sew the furry panda face directly to her flesh.

"Are you okay?" Riley asked her.

He could hear her cringing in pain as she stabbed the needles through her skin.

"Shut up," she told him. "Just be a fucking prisoner back there and shut up."

Julie didn't like people to see her in pain. Even though the kid could only hear her, it was enough to make her uncomfortable. She tried to hold off the pain so that the kid wouldn't notice, but the agony became far too unbearable once she had to sew the eyeholes of the mask to the tender flesh under her inner eyelids.

Julie's face was in too much pain to sleep, so she opened the hatch on her cockpit and climbed the ladder down the side of her slinky-spider. Before she could reach the bottom, Pepper the sunflower jumped her from behind.

"You don't hate me do you?" Pepper asked.

His voice was so frantic Julie wasn't sure what he had said at first.

"Why would I hate you?" Julie said.

"You were in there for so long I thought maybe you were avoiding me," Pepper said. "Most people don't like me. They say I annoy them and talk too much. I don't talk too much do I?"

Julie tried not to look at the flower's soft round face. Unlike the other plushies, the flower's face didn't have much expression. All it could really do was smile. The mouth on the face didn't even seem to move.

"Maybe a little," Julie said.

"Everyone always ignores me and shuts me out," Pepper said. "They treat me like less of a being. Is it because I don't have organs like everyone else does now? I don't have a heart? Is it because I'm still a machine?" He grabbed his thin stem-like body. His fingers could fit all the way around it. "The doctors say my body won't fit any organs. I can't have the operation. Is that fair? I don't think it's fair. I would have the operation if I could. I'm not less of a being because I don't have organs am I?"

Julie wanted to get away from him as quickly as possible.

"What's so great about organs?" Julie said. "You're better off without them."

"But everyone has them now," said the flower. "Why would I be better off without them?"

Julie quoted the speech Poro gave her as a child, "They get diseased. They rot. You have to take good care of them or else you get sick. They're just a pain in the ass if you ask me."

The flower stopped and thought about it for a second.

Then he said, "You mean… I'm *better* because I don't have organs?"

"Of course you are."

The flower looked off into space. "Hey, yeah… Yeah! If I had organs I'd probably get one of those bacterial infections that everyone keeps getting. I don't want to smell like rotten meat. I'm a flower. I'm supposed to smell pretty!"

While the flower was busy being excited about his fresh-smelling petals, Julie used the opportunity to sneak away from him. She walked along the edge of the plateau and found a quiet place to sit, away from the others.

"Damn…" Julie said when she had the chance to breathe in the view.

The sky was pink and orange as the sun was setting behind the skeletal city. She hadn't seen a sunset in a very long time. She had forgotten about sights such as this, spending far too much of her life hiding underground and focused on survival.

"It's beautiful, isn't it?" said a gruff voice behind her.

Julie looked back to see the kangaroo perched on a tall rock. She just nodded a response and went back to taking in the view.

"It makes all of it worthwhile," he said. "All the shit we've had to endure. All the horrible atrocities we've had to commit. It all comes into perspective when you sit back and admire the natural beauty of the world we've inherited."

Julie nodded as he spoke.

"Now that it's all ours, we've got to do right by it," he continued. "That's what General Griz always told me."

The Captain paused for a moment to light up a cigarette.

"I know you all think I'm crazy for putting so much importance in Old Griz," he said. "But it's not just because he's done so much for our kind. It's personal. That bear has been like a father to me."

The kangaroo took a drag off his cigarette and let out a long exhalation.

Then he continued, "Don't get me wrong. I know perfectly well that Griz is a motherfucker. Everyone knows how that guy can get. But if you knew the side of him that I know, you might understand the old bastard. Deep down, that son of a bitch has more heart than any toy I've ever known."

Julie felt uneasy hearing all of this. She planned to kill the teddy bear herself if he didn't die on his own before they left the badlands. She didn't need to hear about his redeeming qualities. The General was a monster and deserved what was coming to him.

"You see, Griz knows these times are cruel," said the kangaroo. "And he knows he's a product of these times. But he believes it's going to take cruelty in order to secure a bright future for our species. That's why he does what he does. It's all for the future of our kind."

The kangaroo stood up.

"I heard what you three were saying back there," said the Captain. "Those were some treasonous words."

Julie froze, amazed that he heard them conspiring against him from across the hill. He had to have been thirty yards away when they had that conversation.

"I completely understand why you'd want to kill me before I killed you," he said. His voice was completely calm and unthreatening. "I'd do the same. But that doesn't change anything. The deal still stands."

He jumped down from the rock. Julie clicked the safety off of her machine gun, preparing herself to shoot him if he came any closer.

"You probably saved my life back there," said the kangaroo. "And I'm grateful. That's why I'm giving you this warning."

Julie turned to point her rifle at the kangaroo, but he leapt at her faster than she could blink. He seized the barrel of her weapon in his fluffy claws and pointed it over his shoulder.

"If you do come after me," he said, staring directly in her goggles, "I'll know you're coming."

Then he let go of her weapon and hopped backward, over the column of rocks toward the horses.

As Julie sat there, trying to catch her breath, she wondered how the hell such a toy as Captain Caw had ever been created. He was able to disarm her within an instant, with his bare hands, from fifteen feet away. She wondered if it wouldn't have been best to have left him to the Whiners back there.

As Julie stood and brushed dirt from her plushy fur, three toys crawled up the side of the hill toward her. They were plastic teeth the size of shoeboxes. They walked toward her on thin noodley legs, smiling at her with tiny cartoon faces.

She backed away, gripping her machine gun. Behind her, there were even more of them. She was surrounded. They came up the hill by the dozen, almost dancing as they walked, making giggly gurgling noises that chilled Julie to her human bones.

CHAPTER SIX

Young Julie shrieked when she saw them. Strapped into the dentist's chair, her gums numb with Novocain, she watched in horror as four plastic teeth-shaped smart-toys danced across the table in front of her, singing about proper dental care.

"Get them away from me!" she cried. "Get them away!"

The dancing teeth looked at her with their terrifying cartoon faces—pointy eyebrows, black dot eyes, and smiling mouths that did not move to the correct rhythm of their words.

"What's wrong?" the dentist asked.

Julie's mother ran into the dentist's office, "What's going on? What happened?"

"Scary!" Julie cried, pointing at the singing teeth.

The teeth did not react. They continued to sing and smile as they danced.

"They're not scary," said the dentist. "They want to teach you about flossing and brushing your teeth."

He picked one up off the table.

"They're cute," he said. "Look."

He shoved the wiggling tooth into Julie's face and she screamed at the top of her lungs.

"No!" she screamed. "Get it away!"

The doctor returned the tooth to the others.

Her mother just laughed at Julie's behavior.

"I'm sorry," she told the dentist. "She's just being a baby."

Julie struggled to get out of the dentist's chair.

"They're trying to eat my soul!" she cried. "Don't let them eat my soul!"

The dentist and Julie's mother just laughed at her and patted her on the head as the singing teeth crawled up her legs onto her lap and proceeded to brush her teeth with a dancing demonic toothbrush.

The memory had been buried deep down in Julie's psyche, but seeing the singing teeth once again filled her with panic. She backed away as they came up the hill toward her, singing and dancing on their noodle legs. She tripped over a rock and fell backward, losing her machine gun in the tumble.

She was paralyzed by fear as the toy teeth jumped on her stomach and began to dance, singing about dental hygiene. Before they could proceed to brush her teeth, Julie pulled her shotgun out from behind her back and aimed it at the closest toy.

The tooth brushed the barrel of the shotgun just before Julie pulled the trigger and blasted the thing into a cloud of tiny white specks.

The teeth didn't try to flee. As she stood up, the teeth danced around her ankles. One of them hugged her foot.

"Get away," she cried, and pulled the trigger.

She continued firing on the dancing teeth until her shotgun was empty. Then she took off, running across the plateau back to the others.

When she arrived, the three plushies just stared at her.

"What the hell are you doing?" Velvet asked.

There were teeth dancing and singing around their legs, but the plushies weren't doing anything about them. That's when Julie finally realized the teeth weren't a threat. They were just trying to teach them about proper dental care.

"Let's go," said Captain Caw. "If this singing hasn't drawn attention to our location those gunshots certainly did."

Julie felt stupid for panicking, but she decided not to say anything in her defense.

"Thanks a lot, psycho," Velvet said. "I was having the best dream before you woke me up with your shooting."

Julie just crawled into her slinky-spider and ignored her, but as soon as she closed the hatch on her cockpit she realized what the bunny woman had just said.

"Wait a minute," she said to herself. "Smart-toys can dream?"

They now had the organs of living beings, including organic brains, but the ability to dream? Where did that come from?

As Julie followed the others in her slinky-spider, she tried not to look at all the singing teeth they passed on their descent down the hill.

"Not all of the toys are dangerous," Riley told her from the back of the horse. "A lot of them moved into the badlands in order to escape the war, unable to choose sides."

Riley knocked on the door of his cell to get her attention.

"Like those wacky wallwalkers over there," he said.

Julie looked back to see the boy was pointing at giant red octopus-looking toys sliding down the side of an old office building. There were seven of them, wrapping their sticky tentacles around the buildings like something out of a Japanese monster movie.

"Or that jack-in-the-box," Riley said.

Poking out of a pile of rubble, Julie saw a clown head bobbing side-to-side on a spring. Then five more jack-in-the-box heads popped out of old car tires and discarded toilet seats, bouncing at them as if saying hello.

"Not all of them are your enemy," Riley said. "Many of them are just trying to survive out here in the wasteland."

"You sound as if you feel bad for them," Julie said.

"I feel bad for everything living in this world," the kid said. "My father always said that it doesn't matter what happens anymore. Everything's fucked for everyone forever."

"Sounds like a great guy."

"He was."

Julie could tell the boy was smiling, remembering his time with his father. She didn't have the heart to tell him that she was just being sarcastic.

For the next ten miles through the badlands, they only came across frightened toys that ran away whenever the slinky-spiders moved toward them. The toys seemed like wild animals, like raccoons digging through the city trash. The sun was down but it wasn't completely dark yet. They could still see where they were going.

"So what else is out here besides these scavenger toys?" Julie asked her prisoner. "Is there anything worse than the Whiners?"

"Much worse," Riley said.

Julie picked at the collection of scabs beneath her plushy skin, watching a swarm of tiny glowing fairies flying through the drive-thru of an old McDonald's restaurant.

"My father said the Whiners are only the third most dangerous tribe in the badlands," Riley said. "Even more dangerous are the Stomps and the Mad Markers."

"What are they like?" Julie asked.

"Well, the names pretty much describe what they're like," Riley said. "They call them Stomps because they're huge and crush anything they come across. And the Mad Markers are just complete psychos. They are the most dangerous tribe by far. But they aren't the most dangerous because they are the most powerful; they are the most dangerous because they are the most sadistic. They love to kill."

"What do they look like?" Julie asked. "Will I recognize them if I see them?"

"They're hard to miss. They wear human flesh as clothing, and use human bones and skulls for armor. They also eat the humans they capture."

"They're cannibals?"

"Can you call toys that eat humans cannibals?" Riley said. "Unlike the plushies, they've never had the operation to implant organs inside their bodies, so they don't even need to eat in order to survive. They eat human flesh just for the fun of it, while the human is still alive."

"Fucking hell…" Julie said.

"But don't worry," he said. "Mad Marker territory is in the opposite direction. It's the Stomps I'm more worried about."

"They're big, you said?" Julie asked.

"They're huge."

"Does that mean we'll see them coming from far away?"

"It doesn't matter if we see them coming," Riley said. "If we come anywhere near a Stomp we're dead."

"You said the same thing about the Whiners and we got through there okay."

"That's because I didn't know this thing could jump so high. That worked for escaping the Whiners, but there's no jumping away from a Stomp. It would just knock you out of the air like a fly."

Captain Caw slowed down in the thick mud and then stopped at a junction up ahead. Julie's slinky-spider was at the back of the convoy, so she couldn't tell what was going on. The sun was down and there wasn't much moonlight through the thick fog. Their vehicles' headlights didn't reach very far.

"What's going on?" Riley said.

The kangaroo was outside of his medical horse. The others were pulling their horses over to speak to him.

"I can't tell," Julie said. "They look worried."

When she made it to them, she told Riley to sit tight and climbed out of the cockpit of the black sphere. A cloud of light gray moths swarmed her like a lamp post.

"Turn the lights out," Velvet yelled up at her.

Julie did as she was told before she climbed down.

In the darkness, she went to the others to figure out what was going on. They spoke in low voices, fully aware of the dangerous territory they were in.

"What's wrong?" Julie asked them.

The other plushies looked at each other, then looked away. "It's the General," said the kangaroo. "He's lost too much blood. He won't make it in time."

"How long does he have?"

"I'm not a medic, but he doesn't look good. He's hardly breathing."

Pepper was quiet and kept his distance from the others. The flower was terrified of what the Captain would do to him if the teddy bear died.

"Can't we give him a blood transfusion ourselves?" Velvet asked.

The kangaroo shook his head. "We don't have the equipment. The medical horse lost a lot of supplies in Whiner territory."

"What about a human hospital?" Velvet asked. "There's got to be one around here somewhere. It could have the equipment we'd need."

"Maybe," said the Captain. "But the few human hospitals that are still standing have probably been picked clean by scavengers by now. Besides, I wouldn't know how to do a blood transfusion, would you?"

Velvet looked down and shook her head.

"I might," Julie said.

They looked at her.

"I've seen one done before," she said. "I might be able to do the job if I had the right equipment and the right blood."

Julie had seen dozens of blood transfusions, actually. She spent so much time in the doctor's cabin while going through surgery that she witnessed all kinds of medical procedures.

"Are you serious?" Velvet asked.

"I can't promise anything but I can try," Julie said. "That is, if I have a matching blood donor."

"I have the same blood type," said the kangaroo.

"Then get me to the hospital and I'll see what I can do," Julie said.

Velvet looked over at the Captain. "It sounds like our best hope."

The kangaroo grunted in agreement. Then he stepped into

Julie's face.

"I'll find you a hospital," he said. "But you'll do more than just *try*. You will succeed or you'll be the first one I execute."

Then the Captain climbed back into the medical horse and turned east. He led them deeper into the badlands, into what was once the downtown area of the lifeless metropolis. And once Riley knew where they were headed, he told Julie they were going directly into the heart of Stomp territory.

It wasn't the Captain who found them a hospital. It was Pepper. Before the war, smart-toy flowers like Pepper were often given to sick children in the hospital instead of real flowers. It was a way to cheer them up and keep them company during long hospital stays. Pepper had spent three weeks in this particular hospital, during which he had been given to four different patients.

"It was fun cheering up the sick kids," Pepper said. "But they always died on me eventually. That wasn't so much fun."

The hospital building was mostly still intact when they arrived, but the insides seemed mostly empty. Gutted.

"Wait here," the Captain told everyone outside of the emergency room entrance. "Keep an eye on the General while I make sure the building is clear."

As he went for the entrance, Pepper kicked an old pipe across the cracked asphalt. It caused a clanging noise to echo through the street.

"And keep quiet," said the Captain. "This is not a friendly area."

Then he disappeared into the darkness of the hospital.

"Not a friendly area?" Velvet said, looking over at Julie. "Talk about the absolute worst possible area. Downtown in the badlands? We're just asking to be slaughtered."

"It's quiet so far," Julie said.

"It won't be for much longer," said Velvet. "Don't let your guard down for a second." Then she looked over at Pepper.

"Especially not you, flower-brain."

Then she tossed a pebble at him and it bounced off his cushy round face.

Captain Caw was taking way too long inside of the hospital.

"Do you think we should go in and get him?" Velvet asked.

Julie shrugged.

"What if he's dead?" Pepper said. "What if he's dead in there and we're next? What're we gonna do?"

"Relax," Velvet said. "If he's dead that means he won't be able to kill us later."

"Oh yeah…" Pepper said. "Oh yeah!"

Julie leaned against her slinky-spider and watched for signs of movement on the road. Wind blowing against rusty metal created a deep squealing sound. The scurrying of cockroaches was the only movement in the area.

"So what's the plan?" Velvet asked Julie, pacing along the road with her sniper rifle at waist level.

"Plan?" Julie asked.

"It doesn't look hopeful for the General. The second he dies, we need to be ready for Caw. We better come up with a plan. Fast."

"The Captain heard our conversation back there," Julie said. "He knows we'll be coming for him."

Velvet looked at Pepper. Panic spread across the flower's face.

"Well…" Velvet groaned. "Shit…"

"We don't have surprise on our side?" Pepper cried. "Fuck. We have nothing. We're so fucked!"

"We just attack him hard and fast," Julie said. "Don't hesitate. Just shoot him."

"If I can get him in my sights I'd be able to take him out," Velvet said. "But I'll need distance. He might be a master of short range attacks, but I'm a master at long range. I think I can get him."

Julie nodded. "Then that's our plan. When I give you the signal you take off running. I'll try to keep him busy while you find a good position."

"Get him out in the open if you can," Velvet said.

"Are we really doing this?" Pepper said. "Are we really going to try to kill Captain Caw?"

"If the General doesn't pull through," Velvet said. "We won't have a choice."

There were headlights coming down the road toward them. The sound of an engine roared their way.

"Where the hell did that come from?" Velvet said, walking toward the center of the road.

It was only a single pair of headlights from some kind of vehicle driving their way. Julie hadn't seen a working motor vehicle in years. Toys didn't drive them. Neither did humans, anymore.

"There's only one of them, right?" Julie asked.

Velvet nodded.

"It must have been there the whole time, just waiting on the side of the road," Velvet said.

"Who is it?" Pepper asked. "Who could it be?"

Velvet looked through the scope on her sniper rifle, her purple floppy ear dangling over the side of the barrel.

"Whoever it is, they're not going to live to tell their friends about us," Velvet said.

Getting the driver in her scope, Velvet fired. She lowered her gun, waited.

"Nothing?" Pepper asked.

Velvet loaded another round and fired again. Then three more times. The vehicle did not stop.

"It's not bulletproof," Velvet said. "The bullets are going through the windshield. The driver should be dead."

When it came closer, Julie and Velvet backed away from

the road. It was a large tanker truck. A big rig. Julie hadn't seen one of those in a decade. She wondered who the heck could be driving it.

"Pepper, get ready," Velvet told the flower, but Pepper was already pulling explosives from his case.

The truck slowed down and stopped alongside the hospital. The vehicle was old and rusted. Only faint chips of yellow remained of its paint job. Weeds grew in and out of the metal, like it had just come out of a junk yard after rotting there since the 1970s. Julie was amazed the thing was still working.

The plushies pointed their weapons at the cab of the truck, waiting for something to happen. But the truck just stayed in its spot, motionless, the engine rumbling.

Velvet approached the rig and looked inside the cab. The windshield was full of bullet holes. The seats were covered in shards of glass. Nobody was inside of it.

She backed away and said, "Who the hell was driving this thing?"

"Is it a trap?" Pepper cried. "What if it's a trap? Should I blow it up?"

"The thing must be haunted," Julie said, backing toward her slinky-spider.

A hand grabbed her fur from behind. She turned to see Riley reaching through the bars.

"Get out of here right now," Riley whispered to her. She could tell by the look in his eyes that he was terrified of that truck. "That thing's a Stomp."

The second Julie looked back, the rusty tanker truck opened up into thirty sections which twisted and turned like a rubik's cube.

"What the hell's happening?" Julie asked.

But Velvet seemed to know exactly what was coming next as she ran back to her slinky-spider.

When the truck was finished transforming, what was standing in the road was a man-shaped machine. A rusted giant junkyard robot with jagged black metal fists.

"A smart-morpher?" Julie said to Riley. "You never said the Stomps were smart-morphers."

Smart-morphers were one of the main reasons the toys won the war against the humans. They were based on an old toy line called Transformers, but these toys could transform on their own. They could think and drive and fight bad guys. But it wasn't until they constructed life-sized smart-morphers that they became really dangerous.

The giant robot roared like a mechanical gorilla and punched its fist into the ground, creating a crater-sized hole in the street that rumbled the ruins for a mile in every direction. It was a battle cry that all of its friends in the region surely heard.

"Forget about the Captain," Velvet yelled from her slinky-spider. "Let's just get the hell out of here." Then her slinky legs launched her into the air.

But the bunny wasn't fast enough. The robot stomped forward and punched the black sphere out of the sky like a tennis ball, sending her flying over the hospital with a crushed cockpit. If she wasn't killed on impact the fall would have surely ended her.

Julie climbed up the ladder to get to her cockpit, but the morpher was too fast. Before she could even get into the driver's seat, she saw the robot's ten-ton foot coming down on top of her. Just one stomp and she would be crushed.

"Over here, fatty!" Pepper cried up at the robot.

There was an explosion and the morpher tumbled backward, away from Julie.

"How about another one!"

Julie looked back to see Pepper launching mortars up at the robot. The flower barely looked like he could lift the rockets with his spindly green limbs, but he was an expert marksman. Every rocket he launched hit the morpher directly in the chest or face.

Although the blasts were not powerful enough to take down the robot, they were enough to immobilize it. The thing couldn't retaliate with the explosions pushing it backward into the crumbling buildings across the street.

"Everyone should start calling me Fire Flower!" Pepper yelled. He cackled at the robot in his high-pitched jittery voice, and then launched another mortar. "I can blow up anything. Anything!" His flower petals flapped wildly as he jittered with psychotic laughter. "I'll blow up *you!*"

While the robot was pressed up against the building, plaster and shrapnel crumbling over its shoulders, Pepper took a moment to get out his big explosive. It was a rocket with ten times as much fire power as the others.

"I'll blow you up until you die!" Pepper said, as he loaded the rocket and aimed it directly for the robot's face.

As the mortar was launched, the robot's head folded back into its body. The rocket missed its target, passing through the crumbling building, and exploded in the ruins twenty yards away.

Regaining itself, the morpher pulled itself from the collapsing building, unfolded its head from its body, and stomped across the street toward the flower.

"Get out of there," Julie yelled.

Pepper squealed, trying to load another rocket, but the robot was faster. Its massive foot came crashing down on top of the flower before the last round could be fired.

Then it turned toward Julie.

"Fuck..." Julie said, hopping out of the slinky-spider cockpit.

As the robot raised its foot to crush her vehicle, Julie looked up at it. She could see Pepper flat against its foot, shaking and squealing. He was still alive, clinging to the metal with his life. The flower had such a thin wiry body that he was able to fit inside the cracks of the robot's foot without being crushed.

"Come on," she yelled at Riley, opening the hatch to his cell.

She pulled the boy out of the back just as the robot's foot crushed the black sphere into the ground. They rolled back into the street. There was nothing left of the slinky-spider but a flattened black mass of metal.

"You saved me?" Riley said.

A look of surprise was on his face, as if he never expected she would do anything for anybody but herself.

"I still need you, remember," she said. But the boy smiled and thanked her anyway.

When the robot turned to them, Julie saw Pepper crawling up its leg like a fuzzy green spider.

"What's he doing?" Riley asked.

Pepper laughed hysterically as he crawled into the morpher's torso, through its inside machinery, placing small round disks in all of its vital areas.

"He's planting mines," Julie said. "Run."

Julie took off running down the street with the boy, trying to find cover. When she looked back, she saw Pepper crawling up the robot's face.

"Boop!" Pepper said, as he planted his last mine on the tip of the robot's nose.

The smart-morpher jerked its head, shaking the flower off of its face. Pepper giggled madly as he fell through the air. Then he raised his hand to show the robot the detonator he was holding.

The machine's eyes brightened red. It looked at its body, searching for the mines, but there was nothing it could do in time. Pepper pushed the button on his detonator and the robot exploded. Chunks of flaming metal crumbled to the ground.

Riley and Julie jumped behind a slab of concrete as shrapnel rained from the sky. She wrapped her plushy arms around the boy and held him tightly, protecting him from the falling debris. When it was all over, the robot was nothing but a flaming pile of junk in the road.

"Are you okay?" Julie asked, helping Riley out from under their cover.

Riley nodded. Then he smiled at her and rubbed her furry panda belly.

"You're soft," he said.

She smacked his hand away and stepped forward, pointing

at something in the distance.

"What's that?" she said.

Riley squinted his eyes. There were dozens of headlights shining their way.

"Stomps," Riley said. "An entire army of them."

"It took that much to kill one and now we have to face a dozen more?"

"It looks like two or three dozen to me," Riley said.

They turned and marched back toward the hospital.

"Wait…" Riley said.

He paused and listened. There was a sound coming from the distance and it wasn't just the roaring sounds of engines.

"It sounds like screaming," Julie said.

There were riders inside of the vehicles coming their way, screaming with excitement.

"It's not just the Stomps," Riley said. "The Mad Markers are with them too."

He squinted his eyes at the distance.

"What?" Julie said.

"It's almost as if…" He stared at Julie with a terrified expression. "They've joined forces."

Julie looked back to see the army heading their way. The two most deadly tribes in the badlands were now one. And Julie just happened to be in the center of their territory.

CHAPTER SEVEN

Julie and Riley ran back toward the hospital. Along the way, they came across Pepper who was pulling himself to his feet.

"I told you I could blow up anything," he told Julie with a cartoon smile on his face.

"Can you blow up that?" Julie asked, pointing at the army coming their way.

The smile fell from the flower's face. "Oh fuck…"

He followed them as they went toward the slinky-spiders. Only two of them remained: the medical horse and the one Pepper was riding. Julie looked at the horses, then looked back at the army of smart-morphers, then at Pepper.

"Should we just run for it?" Julie asked Pepper.

Pepper nodded ten times rapid-fast.

"Hell yeah let's run for it," he cried. "Let's get as far as we fucking can and never look back ever again for as long as we live."

But even though he said that, Pepper couldn't move. He just stared at the back of the medical horse, hesitating.

"Everyone okay down there?" said a voice from the roof.

Julie looked up to see Velvet up there holding her sniper rifle, standing on top of the hospital as if that's where she was meant to be.

"You're still alive?" Julie asked.

Velvet spit over the side. "I jumped out in time with only a few bumps and bruises. Can't say the same for the human prisoner riding in the back, though. His guts were sprayed halfway across the badlands."

"You see what's coming our way?" Julie asked.

Velvet looked over her shoulder toward the lights in the distance.

"Looks like a whole hell of a lot of trouble," she said.

"We're thinking of running," Julie said.

"There's no running from that," Velvet said.

Then Captain Caw marched out of the hospital toward them. When Riley saw the kangaroo coming, he ducked behind the flower's horse.

"Nobody's running," said the Captain.

"Where the hell were you?" Julie asked him.

"Finding your equipment," said the kangaroo. "It's time you got started."

Then he looked up at Velvet.

"Be ready for them," he told her. "Hold that position for as long as you can."

Then he said, "Here, catch," as he tossed an ammunition bag up to her. She caught it with her left paw.

"Explosive rounds?" she asked, when she looked into the bag.

"You're going to need them," he said.

Then he looked at the flower.

"Before they get here, I want you to set up a minefield in front of the hospital and a tripwire in the entrance," he told Pepper. "Then find a safe spot to hit them with rockets. Change your position every two shots you take."

He looked at Julie.

"You just focus on the General," he told her. "Keep him alive at all costs."

"What are you going to do?" Julie asked the Captain.

"After you take my blood, I'm going to kill every single one of those bastards myself."

Then the Captain went to the back of the medical horse to check on the General. The massive teddy bear was still alive back there, gasping for air. Julie wasn't sure what she should do about the General. Whether she saved him or let him die, they both had unfavorable outcomes.

There was a sobbing noise in Julie's ear. She turned to see a figure inside the cell on the back of Pepper's slinky-spider. Upon closer inspection, Julie noticed the prisoner inside was a young girl no older than six. She had raggedy blonde hair and bloody bandages covering her eye sockets. It was clear the girl had been recently blinded.

While the others weren't paying attention, Julie went to Riley and whispered to him, "Once we're out of sight, I want you to free her from this cell. Then I want you to take her and find a good hiding spot out in the waste. Keep her safe until it's over."

Riley didn't say anything in response. He just nodded with conviction. He understood perfectly well what he needed to do.

Julie and Captain Caw wheeled the enormous teddy bear through the moonlit hospital, passing cobwebbed skeletons and dust-caked debris. They took a few ramps up to the third floor, where there was a semi-clean operating room ready for them. The place was lit by a single oil lamp the kangaroo had set up.

"This far away?" Julie asked. "Couldn't you have found something closer by?"

"This place is the most secure," said the Captain.

They wheeled him in and Julie went to work immediately.

"Roll up your sleeve and show me your arm," she said.

This was the part she wanted to finish as quickly as possible. Getting blood from Captain Caw wasn't going to be easy. She didn't like being that close to him. She wanted him out in the battle.

The kangaroo glared at her with his red bulging eyes as he rolled up his black leather sleeve. She took his arm and examined it. His meat was so loose and pliable under the fur. She had no idea how she was going to find a vein.

"What's taking you so long?" he asked, after five minutes of examining his arm.

A bomb exploded in the street outside of the window, signaling the start of the battle. The morphers had arrived.

"I can't find your vein," Julie said.

The kangaroo pulled his arm out of Julie's hands. He brought it up to his lips and bit into it. Blood splashed at Julie as he ripped open his flesh, opening up the plushy hide of his forearm. When he was through removing his skin, Julie could see the muscles, tendons and veins pulsating before her.

"Can you find it now?" asked the kangaroo.

Julie just nodded at him, then stuck the syringe into his vein. Minutes later, she had a full blood pack.

"That's it," she said. "I can take it from here."

The Captain dropped a bag of extra ammo by her feet. Shotgun shells.

"When you're done with him, guard the hallway," he said. "I'll do everything I can to keep them out of the building, but there are a lot of entrances to this place. Some will likely get inside."

"Aren't they too big to get in?" Julie asked.

"I'm not talking about the big ones," he said. "The short guys are the ones you'll have to worry about."

Then the Captain drew his samurai swords and took off down the hallway, leaving her alone with the massive red teddy bear.

Julie went to the window to investigate what the kangaroo meant by the short guys. The Mad Markers was what the boy called them, but she had to see what they were up against for herself.

Down below, in the streets outside, dozens of cars and trucks were transforming into giant robots, smashing through buildings and piles of rubble, trying to track down the plushy soldier who kept firing bombs at them. But some of them did not transform. They kept their vehicle shape so that they could transport their passengers into the battlefield.

As a group of crazed warriors jumped out of the back of a truck, Julie got a good look at them. The Mad Markers were only two or three feet high, screaming high-pitched battle cries and waving hand-made axes carved from rusty scrap metal. They wore human skulls for helmets and had chest-armor made of human bones sewn into human flesh hides. But what grabbed Julie's attention most of all was what was beneath their flesh and bone clothing.

Their hard plastic bodies were brightly colored. Some green, some blue, some pink, some yellow, but each of them had white bellies containing a unique marking. Julie recognized some of the markings: a heart, a rainbow, a cupcake. Before the war, Julie was very familiar with the toy line that became the Mad Markers.

"Carebears?" Julie said. "They're fucking Carebears?"

She watched in horror as the Carebear warriors charged toward the hospital, growling and shrieking, their eyes glowing bright red as they gnashed their razor sharp metal teeth.

Julie fell to the floor as the earth shook around her. She staggered into the hallway and saw the entire west wing of the hospital being ripped away.

Outside, all she saw of what caused the destruction was a metal hand the size of a house brushing past the opening. The sound of its stomping feet thundered through the building. She wasn't sure what that morpher had been before it transformed into a giant robot, but it must have been an aircraft carrier or a skyscraper. If it wanted to, it probably could take out the whole building itself.

Luckily, it was not after her yet. It was after Pepper the sunflower. She couldn't see the flower out in the darkness, but she saw his pyrotechnics. He was lighting up the badlands with flaming robots, transforming them into heaps of fiery scrap metal. The massive skyscraping morpher wasn't going to be so easy for him, though. He would need a megaton bomb to take that one out.

Julie decided to forget about the battle being waged outside. She had business to attend to, with the General.

"Ugly raping motherfucker," Julie said to the teddy bear as she approached his charred bandaged body. "Now what am I going to do with you?"

She went to his bed and stared down at him.

"I really should kill you," she said. "But that would mean your buddy, Captain Caw, would come after me."

She held up the blood pack. It was still warm and squishy.

"I could give you this blood as I told the others I would," she said. "But if you wake up and tell them about me they'll figure out what I really am."

She set the blood pack down and went around to the back of his bed, looking down at his fluffy skull.

"Maybe there's a way I can damage your brain," she said, holding his massive head in her plushy hands. "Not enough to kill you. Just enough so that you'll never think an intelligent thought ever again. I'm sure the Captain will never know."

Julie picked up an old scalpel from the counter and brought it to his skull.

"I'll just remove the tiniest piece and see what happens," she said. "Hopefully, it won't kill you."

As Julie pressed the scalpel against the teddy bear's head, a deep moan escaped from his lungs. Then she saw movement under his bandages.

She cut the gauze off of his chest and saw that the movement was underneath his skin. Five little bumps appeared on his torso. Something was crawling inside him.

"What the fuck?" Julie said.

She brought the scalpel toward one of the bumps, wondering if she should cut him open to see what was inside. The bump moved across his flesh toward one of the bullet holes on his torso.

When it arrived at the hole, it disappeared. Julie pulled the scalpel away, wondering what the hell that was all about.

Then a tiny smart-soldier popped out of his wound and screamed in a high-pitched voice, "Surprise!"

Julie dropped to the ground as the tiny soldier opened fire. She crawled across the room, covering her head with her paws.

Four more tiny green soldiers popped out of his bullet holes and fired at Julie.

She crawled into the hallway and rolled around the corner, leaning against the wall to catch her breath.

"What the fuck was that?" she said.

Now she understood why the Whiners were considered masters of the ambush. All this time, those little fuckers were hiding in the bear's wounds, waiting for a chance to strike.

Julie didn't have time for this. She had to take care of those little soldiers and deal with General Griz before the Captain came back for her. She was going to have to pull them out of him one by one.

She ran back into the operating room and hit the ground. Their miniature bullets sprayed across the wall behind her.

"Okay, you big fucker, time to get your parasites removed," she said as she crawled across the floor.

When she arrived at the tray holding the surgical equipment, she knocked it over. Grabbing the tongs and using the tray as a shield, she stood up.

"Is that all you've got you little pricks?" she said, holding the tray in front of her to protect her face and torso.

Their tiny bullets couldn't pierce the tray as she marched slowly toward them. Once she was only a foot away, hovering above the bear's torso, she attacked. Using the pair of surgical tongs, she grabbed one of them and pulled him out of the bullet hole like a maggot from a wound.

The tiny soldier wiggled and squirmed in the air until Julie tossed him across the room. His little green body cracked into pieces when he hit the wall.

"Who's next?" she told the other soldiers.

As she said that, the other four smart-soldiers dropped down inside of the wounds, burrowing into the flesh like gopher tunnels.

"You motherfuckers," she said, digging her tongs into one

of the holes.

As she stuck the metal pliers deep inside, a loud groan came out of the bear. She looked up at him. His eyes were opening. He was gaining consciousness.

Once awake, General Griz lifted his head and saw Julie standing over him with the pair of tongs shoved inside of his stomach. There was a moment of pause as they just stared at each other—both of them contemplating how the hell they got into that situation.

Then the recognition flashed through the teddy bear's eyes. "You..." he roared.

He lunged off of the operating table at Julie. She fell backward onto the floor, watching the gigantic red teddy bear as he pulled himself to his feet.

"You traitor," he said in a crackling electric voice, towering over her.

The bandages fell off of his face to reveal horribly charred flesh. Half of his skull poked through his blackened plushy head.

As he staggered toward her, the four smart-soldiers poked out of his bullet wounds and fired at Julie. Griz didn't even seem to realize they were in there as he stomped forward.

Julie ran across the room and out into the hallway, shutting the door behind her. The bear slammed against it, cracking the wood to splinters.

Now that half of the hospital had been torn down—the sound of gunfire and explosions coming from outside—Julie only had one place left to run. But as soon as she took two steps in that direction, she saw a horde of snarling Carebears charging down the hallway toward her.

"You've got to be shitting me," Julie said, as the screaming Carebears raised their axes.

Then the giant teddy bear burst through the splintered door.

CHAPTER EIGHT

The hallway was dark but for the light of explosions coming from outside.

Julie whipped the shotgun off of her back and went for the Carebears first. She was well-trained for hitting multiple targets. If she could take them out first then she would only have to worry about the General.

As she charged at the ferocious little flesh-eaters, she tried to think of them as nothing but targets, as glass bottles and nothing more. There were five of them, teeth gnashing and axe-blades squealing as they cut along the gritty plaster walls.

"Feast on her flesh! Feast on her flesh!" screamed the Carebears in joyful high-pitched voices.

She fired the shotgun three times in a row, pumping and firing just as she trained. The bursts took off one Carebear's head and hit the other two in their chests. They had hard plastic skin, but were hollow inside.

After the shells opened up their inner cavity, a noxious gas filled the hall. Julie caught one breath of the fumes and fell to the ground, gagging and dry-heaving at the odor coming out of the broken toys.

Inside of the Carebears were piles of rotting meat—flesh from all of the victims they had eaten. Since the Carebears were not living beings with digestive tracts, the meat they ate just festered in their hollow cavities until it rotted into a sludgy green soup. When Julie shot them, it was like breaking open a seal. All the gas and fumes that had built up from months of decomposition hit her directly in the face. It was enough to knock her to the ground, putting her into a fit of nausea.

The other two Carebears hopped over their fallen brothers and continued toward her. The stench had no effect on them. They had no sense of smell. Julie tried to raise her shotgun as they charged her but the nausea was so overwhelming that all she could do was cough and gag, plastered to the floor.

"She's mine!" General Griz yelled at the two Mad Markers as he charged down the hallway.

The four smart-soldiers inside of the teddy bear's wounds fired at both Julie and the Carebears. She protected her face from their tiny bullets, but several rounds pierced through her back and thighs. They were like six-inch needles stabbing into the muscle.

The Carebears passed Julie and went for the General. They jumped at his knees and bit into the backs of his calves, thrashing like wild pink and blue dogs.

"You traitor!" the teddy bear yelled, dragging the Carebears with him as he stomped down the hallway.

Julie crawled to her feet, covering her nose and mouth to block out the odor. She ran past the bodies oozing with rotten meat and went toward the ramp leading downstairs. There were a dozen more Mad Markers coming up the ramp toward her, attracted by the sound of the shotgun.

She looked back at the hulk of a teddy bear as he staggered toward her. The General didn't even seem to realize the Carebears chewing on his legs or the army men sticking out of his belly.

"Who sent you to kill me, Panda?" Griz yelled. His voice was mostly static. She could barely make out his words.

Julie just stood there for a moment, watching the ferocious plastic animals racing toward her.

"The dolls? The clowns?" He roared. "Are they planning to break the treaty?"

General Griz looked down and finally noticed the plastic critters gnawing at his feet, tearing off chunks of fuzzy flesh. He raised one foot and stomped on the blue Carebear's belly. When it was crushed into the floor, the toy's rotten stomach contents squeezed out through its mouth and eye sockets.

"Or are you just a lousy human sympathizer?" asked the General.

The other Carebear continued chewing on the General's flesh. It had eaten away so much flesh that Julie could clearly see bone.

"I didn't realize there were any human sympathizers among the plushies," Julie said.

She turned and looked back at the General. The way she looked at him, the way she was standing there, her posture, her figure—the teddy bear could see it. He could finally tell that the panda was a human.

"You…" said the General. "How did you?"

Julie smiled behind her mask. "It wasn't easy…"

Anger rose up inside of the bear. He grabbed the pink Carebear on his leg and snapped it in half, tossing its pieces to the side. He roared at the human in panda disguise. Then he came at her.

Julie said, "But it was worth it…"

Then she charged him. She fired a shell into his belly, shredding open a hole of meat. The tiny green soldiers inside of him were blown to pieces. The bear continued forward as if it were nothing.

She only had time to pump her shotgun again before the bear was on top of her. He swung his paw at Julie with enough force to burst her skull open. Blood and tiny soldier pieces rained out of him. But Julie slid across the floor, ducking under his attack, and fired into his leg. The shotgun blast was aimed directly into the wound opened up by the pink Carebear, giving her a clear shot of the bone. The bear's leg from the knee down was blown in half, throwing the General to the floor.

"Just to take you out."

Julie continued down the hallway, leaving the General alive. She went toward the massive hole in the building where the west wing once stood, hoping there would be a way to climb down.

She looked back at the General. He cried out as the army of Mad Markers reached him, jumping on top of his massive bag of flesh. All he could see was a dozen pairs of metal jaws as they bit into him like a school of brightly colored piranha. The yellow Carebear went straight for his jugular, tearing open his throat and drinking his fountain of blood.

They didn't go after Julie, too focused on devouring the

General's flesh into their hollow bodies. She watched until she was sure the teddy bear was dead and wasn't getting back up again. Once she saw the Carebears fighting over his intestines on the floor like a game of tug o' war she knew it was safe to say the giant bastard wasn't coming back to life for a fourth time.

Julie stood on the edge of the collapsed hospital, looking out across the badlands. A cold wind blew through her fuzzy skin, carrying the smell of smoke and rotten innards. The faint sound of explosions and squealing metal trailed off along the breeze.

There were dozens of small fires across the junkyard landscape. Half-transformed trucks and robots lay in fiery pieces. A hundred dead Carebears were like rainbow sprinkles across a nearby dirt lot.

Then she saw Captain Caw.

With his two samurai swords slicing through the wind, he raced through a group of fleeing Mad Markers, cutting them down three at a time. He did so effortlessly, chopping them into halves and quarters. The horrid smell that erupted from within them had no effect on the kangaroo. He was able to kill them and move on before the stench reached his nostrils.

Three large Stomps came at him—a tank, a bulldozer, and a garbage truck. When they reached him, they transformed into robots and attacked. The garbage truck robot hurled a dumpster full of ancient refuse at him, but the Captain cut through it like newspaper. The bulldozer stomped down on him, but he just rolled out of the way. The tank fired its cannon—now positioned on its shoulder like a bazooka—but Captain Caw leapt into the air too quickly, jumping the blast and landing on the tip of the tank-bot's weapon.

He ran up the barrel and stabbed his sword into the robot's face. Then he cut the back of its neck, severing its electronic brain stem. The tank created a thunderous cloud of dust when it fell to the ground.

"Fuck, that guy is strong," Julie said, watching in disbelief from the hospital opening.

Out of the cloud of dust, Captain Caw jumped at the garbage truck robot and sliced through its gas line like a major blood vessel. As the robot staggered back, its fuel gushing out of him, the kangaroo bounced off of the truck's corpse and leapt at the bulldozer robot. He cut through the gas line on his neck like a jugular vein.

As the Captain jumped down from the robot and continued cutting his way through the horde of Carebears, Julie heard a gunshot above her. Then both of the bleeding robots burst into flames and fell to the ground in a heap of burning metal.

It was Velvet who fired. She was still alive up there on the roof with her sniper rifle, firing explosive rounds at the gas-leaking robots. That's where all of the flaming piles of metal had come from. Captain Caw was cutting them down while Velvet was finishing them off.

Julie watched the kangaroo as he took down the last of the Stomps and Mad Markers in the area. Even the giant skyscraper-sized robot was no match for him. It rumbled the ground in front of the hospital as the Captain climbed up its side. Hopping from its leg to its wrist to its chest to its neck, there was nothing the robot could do. Caw was too small and too fast for him.

The Captain entered through the back of the robot's head and cut through cords and wires. The red lights in the giant morpher's eyes went dark. Its head rolled off of its neck with a shower of sparks against its black metal body. In the place of its skull, the Captain stood there with his swords covered in oil and his floppy kangaroo ears blowing in the wind.

"He's a fucking demon," Julie said as she saw the look of bloodlust in his cold soulless eyes. "How the hell am I going to kill something like that?"

Then the robot's body came crashing down. It landed directly in front of the opening on the side of the hospital, sending a wave of debris and smoke into the hallway. Julie hit the floor and covered her face. The robot's hand smashed into the wall just one story down. Just a little higher and it would have swatted her into a pulp.

She looked up. The cloud cleared and Captain Caw walked calmly up the robot's arm toward her. She got to her feet and held out her shotgun. It only clicked when she pulled the trigger. She was out of shells.

The Captain jumped into the hallway with her and looked her in the eyes. He disregarded the gun pointed at his chest.

"How is he?" the Captain asked.

Julie just stood there, staring at the kangaroo. She knew she had only a second or two before he learned about the General's demise. It seemed like now was her only chance to catch the Captain off guard, but he was too close and she wasn't holding the right weapon. She wouldn't be able to get to the MP5 strapped to her back in time. There was nothing she could do.

"What's wrong?" said the Captain.

Julie's lack of response caused a deep emotion to rise inside of the kangaroo. Instead of saying a word, Julie lowered her head and stepped aside.

When the Captain saw his fallen leader on the other side of the hallway, his eyes widened and his jaw went slack. He stepped forward, passing Julie. Then he charged at the Carebears who were devouring Griz.

"More flesh! More flesh!" cried the Carebears.

The enraged Captain sliced at the Mad Markers with bulging red eyes, but he didn't kill any of them. He cut off their arms and legs, stabbed out their eyeballs, opened their bellies. It was almost as if he wanted to wait and finish them off later, when he had time to savor their deaths.

But not killing them quick enough came at a cost. One of the Carebears got through his defenses. As he cut the thing's arms off, it leapt up at him. Its metal teeth dug deep into the Captain's shoulder, creating a blood-filled pit near his neck.

The Captain crushed the Carebear's skull with the handles of his swords and dropped its body into the pile of squirming wounded toys.

Then he looked down at the General. For several minutes,

he just stared. Then he cried.

"Griz..." he said to the body.

He dropped his swords and buried his face in his hands. "Griz..."

Julie didn't think such a killer knew how to cry.

"Nothing matters anymore," said the kangaroo to the dead teddy bear. "The war, the army, the future of our people... there is no future without you, Griz."

He kneeled to the General. His tears rained into his red fur.

"This world means nothing without you," said the kangaroo.

Then he lifted the teddy bear's giant blackened face and kissed him deeply. His tongue entered the corpse's mouth, his tears flowing down both of their cheeks, as he kissed the dead bear with all of his passion.

Julie's mouth dropped open as she watched the kangaroo passionately kissing the dead body.

"What the fuck..." Julie said, as she backed away from the scene.

She climbed down the robot's arm to get out of the hospital and find the others. When she looked back, the Captain was still making out with the dead teddy bear. But now he was getting more into it, wrapping his arms around the corpse and rubbing his guts all over him. Julie was just happy he didn't kill her as promised.

When Julie got to the front of the hospital, she looked everywhere for Riley and the little girl he was protecting. They were nowhere in sight.

"Riley?" she called out.

There wasn't any answer.

She didn't see their bodies anywhere, so she hoped that they got away. Riley seemed to know more about the badlands than anyone she'd ever met, so she figured he would be fine. He would surely know the safest way out of there. He was probably in less danger than Julie at that moment.

"Poro!" cried the flower as he raced out of the rubble toward Julie.

He was frazzled and covered in black ash. Three petals were missing from the side of his head. The sunflower looked like he had been through hell.

"We did it!" he said. "Can you believe it? We took them all out. Just the four of us. Their whole army was obliterated."

Julie wasn't as excited about surviving as he was.

"We should get out of here now," Julie said.

She went toward the slinky-spiders.

"Why?" Pepper asked.

"The General didn't make it," Julie said.

The flower stopped in his tracks and stared at her.

"You mean..." he said.

"The Captain has already seen him," Julie said. "The moment he's finished mourning he'll probably come after us. We should run."

Pepper's remaining petals began shaking on his head.

"But how..." The flower was having a difficult time thinking straight. "What are we going to do?"

Julie kept moving.

"There are only two horses left, right?" she said. "If we take them both he'll have to follow us on foot. That will give us a good head start."

"But he'll hunt us down," Pepper said, grabbing Julie by the arm with his soft noodle fingers. "That's what he's best at— hunting people."

"Would you rather stay here?" Julie asked.

She looked up at the roof and called out for the sniper bunny.

"Velvet," she yelled.

The bunny didn't come to her.

"Velvet?" they both called out.

Pepper looked at Julie. "Is she still alive?"

"I don't know," Julie said. "I thought she was."

"Are you up there?" Julie yelled at the roof.

"We can't wait for her," Pepper said. "We have to go."

"Come on, we're leaving," Julie said to the roof.

Julie shook her head and gave up. As they crossed the road toward the vehicles, something walked out of the hospital entrance toward them. It was the kangaroo, covered in the General's blood. He took slow steps, holding both swords in his hands.

"Nobody's going anywhere," said the Captain.

His eyes were red from crying, but he was already past sadness. Now he was angry.

"We have to run," Julie whispered to the flower.

"No way," Pepper cried.

The Captain continued moving toward them.

"You run left, I run right," she said. "If he gets too close to you, use your explosives. He won't be able to dodge grenades."

The Captain didn't speed up. He just raised his blades to eye level.

"Go!" Julie yelled.

They ran in different directions. The Captain looked left, then he looked right, as if deciding who to go after first.

"I said..." The Captain raised a sword behind his back and looked at the flower as he flopped and wiggled down the road. "Nobody's going anywhere."

He threw the sword. It spun through the air and landed in the back of Pepper's plushy head. A cloud of yellow petals exploded into the air, riding the wind in the direction the flower was heading.

Then the Captain turned to Julie. He had one more sword, just for her.

The kangaroo stalked toward Julie as she ran. He picked up his pace and moved a little quicker, then a little quicker. Then he came to full speed, hopping at Julie with his sword out to his side.

"Hey human," yelled the kangaroo. "You're going to suffer for what you did."

His words caught her off guard. She turned back, wondering how he knew she was human. Did he always know?

As her head was turned, she tripped over robot shrapnel and fell into the street. The kangaroo hopped at full speed toward her. She aimed her MP5 at him and fired. The Captain hopped out of her line of fire, through the wasteland debris, dodging all of her bullets.

"You killed him, you bitch," he yelled. "Nothing in the world will stop me from gutting you."

He threw his sword at Julie. It cut through the barrel of her rifle as she fired, causing an explosion in her hands. Bits of shrapnel hit her chest and arms as it flew behind her.

The kangaroo grabbed her by the throat and ripped her off the ground.

"I'll kill you with my bare hands," he said.

Julie wheezed, trying to pry open his fingers around her neck. Her voice choked out the words, "How did you know?"

He smiled with pointed yellow teeth. Although he had the face of a kangaroo, his jaws were those of a wolf.

"I didn't," he said. "Griz knew."

He pointed at his head.

"I just downloaded his memories so that he and I would become one."

Julie kicked and struggled.

"You didn't know we could do that, did you?" he continued. "Our minds can be removed and put into other bodies. I put Griz's mind into my own."

Julie tried to kick him in the stomach, but the kangaroo

blocked it with his wrist.

He said, "It is illegal to do this, of course. It is illegal to save the mind from one who's been killed. We wouldn't be real living beings if we were allowed to escape death."

He squeezed Julie's throat even tighter. She heard a popping noise in her larynx.

"But I don't care about the laws anymore," said the Captain. "The laws mean nothing to me if I cannot be with my commander. We have become one mind, now. Everything that was him is now within me."

Julie's vision was getting fuzzy. She could feel her mind slipping. But she wasn't going to give up. She couldn't leave her parents in the camps.

She let go of her neck and grabbed at his face with her hand. The kangaroo caught her by the wrist. With no free arms to stop her other hand, Julie dug into the Captain's shoulder wound with her fingernails. The pain shot through his body and he instinctually dropped her. Her fingernails tore open his shoulder flesh as she fell.

"Human bitch," the kangaroo roared.

He looked at the wound on his shoulder. Fresh blood oozed down his leather clothing. Just before he went for Julie, he saw something in the corner of his eye. There was movement inside of his flesh, underneath his wound.

"What the hell..." the kangaroo said, as his wound swelled.

Then a tiny green soldier popped out of his shoulder wound and yelled in a high pitch, "Surprise!"

It fired a burst of miniature bullets into the kangaroo's eyes, blinding him. The smart-soldier had come from the teddy bear. Like a parasite, the little toy escaped its dead host and entered the living one.

The kangaroo jerked his head away from the gunfire and ripped the tiny man out of his wound. As he crushed the toy, Julie went for his samurai sword in the dirt. She pulled it out of the barrel of her MP5 and drove it into his chest.

But even though his eyes had been shredded by tiny bullets, Captain Caw still caught the sword in midair. Only the very tip of the blade broke through his plushy hide.

"This planet doesn't belong to you anymore," the Captain said, squeezing the blade of his sword until fresh blood leaked from his fluffy palm. "Get off."

A gunshot echoed through the ruins. Then a whizzing sound tore through the air and hit Caw in the back of his shoulder blade. The bullet inside of him exploded his shoulder into a splatter of meat and blood.

The arm was the only thing holding Julie back. As the exploding bullet blew the limb to pulp, Julie drove the blade through the Captain's wilted fingers and sliced open his black fuzzy heart.

The Captain gasped once and then slipped down the blade of his own sword. His eyeballs fell from their sockets and hit the mud like acorns falling from an oak tree.

Julie went back toward the hospital entrance and saw Velvet standing there, her sniper rifle draped over her shoulder.

"What took you so long?" Julie asked her.

"I'm pregnant, remember?" The bunny grabbed her swollen purple belly. "It took me forever to climb down from the roof."

They glanced at the yellow and green body in the road.

"He got Pepper," Julie said.

"I noticed."

Julie nodded and then looked at their surroundings. The badlands were quiet. Not a soul left alive.

"I guess it's just the two of us left," Julie said.

The bunny looked at her muddy feet. "Yeah, just us and the prisoners."

Julie's eyes lit up.

"Prisoners?"

Then Velvet pointed to the two children, who were both still alive. They were inside the cage in the back of Pepper's slinky-spider.

"They had gotten out," Velvet said. "But I caught them and put them back. At least we won't be going back completely empty-handed."

Julie's eyes locked with Riley's as he peeked out from the bars. He should have gotten away when he had the chance. Now she was going to have to turn him in to the plushies. She didn't have any other choice.

PART THREE

CHAPTER NINE

Young Julie didn't seem to notice that the halls of her elementary school were so quiet. It was a winter morning, so the sky was still dark outside. Only the emergency lights were operating. Julie could barely make her way through the shadowy building toward her classroom.

Although the elementary school seemed completely empty, it was not as empty as Julie's heart. She had just lost her Poro the night before. After he escaped into the night, Julie cried herself to sleep. She woke up feeling so drained that her head floated separately from her body as she got ready for school.

Nothing much mattered to her at the moment. Her parents didn't believe her when she said Poro ran away. They thought she was hiding him somewhere and tore apart her whole room. The lecture started at breakfast and would not stop for the rest of the morning. When they dropped Julie off that day, they were too busy yelling at her to notice what was clearly wrong with the school.

Julie arrived at her classroom, but it was even darker in there than out in the hall. There were only four other kids inside. They sat quietly at their desks in the shadows. One of them was whispering to a friend. Julie went to her desk in the third row and tossed her backpack under the chair. She put her face in her hands the second she sat down, sobbing, wishing Poro was with her at that moment. She couldn't believe that he was really gone forever.

After half an hour, Julie wiped her eyes and looked up. One other student had arrived after her, but the teacher was nowhere in sight. Class should have started a long time ago.

"Where is everybody?" Julie asked the people in the shadows.

The other kids were silent.

"Is everyone out sick?"

Julie stood up and went to one of the students. As she

approached the girl she could make out what appeared to be blond braided hair and a red dress. Julie wondered who she was. She didn't look like anyone from her class.

"Hello?" Julie asked the girl with the braids.

When she saw who was sitting there, she realized it was not a girl at all. It was a child-sized doll. Julie went to the next kid and realized he too was just a doll. They were smart-dolls, the kinds that were supposed to have been recalled that day.

"What are you doing here?" Julie said.

The dolls did not respond, just staring at the chalkboard.

Julie wondered if she was supposed to have had the day off that day. She wondered if she should just go back home.

On the way out of the room, she passed a boy lying with his head on his desk. It was not a doll, but a human boy. She recognized him. He was a kid named Evan who always came to school early and left late in order to avoid the bullies in his neighborhood.

"Evan?" she said.

When she touched his shoulder, he was cold. There was blood on his desk. Somebody had cut his throat.

Julie looked back and saw the dolls were no longer in their seats. They were in the aisles, walking silently toward her, staring at her with cold plastic faces.

Julie ran out of her classroom and into the hallway. That's when she noticed the bodies. Two children half her age lay folded together in the corner. In the doorway to the boy's bathroom, there was a janitor missing his head. Seven dolls were spread out across the walkway, moving like the undead toward her.

Julie couldn't scream. She could hardly grasp what was happening here.

The dolls pointed butcher knives at her.

"Come play with us," one of them said in an electronic high-pitched whisper. "We need more toys to play with."

"Be our toy," the rest of them said in unison.

Julie ran in the other direction, turned the corner and went into the school office. A baby doll was on the reception desk, stabbing the woman who sat there.

The baby looked back at Julie. Its eyes were missing from their sockets. Its face covered in mold as if it had just come out of the garbage dump.

"Baby wants mommy," it said in its crackling electric voice. Then it stabbed the woman again. "Baby wants mommy."

As Julie went for the door outside, she heard the human woman gagging. Julie realized she was still alive, reaching out with her hand as the baby stabbed her repeatedly.

When Julie's eyes met hers, she panicked. It was at that moment that she realized all of this was real. Blood oozed out of the woman's mouth as she reached for Julie. But Julie could do nothing to help her. She ran out of the building and kept on running. She never looked back.

Outside, the world was in a panic. Cars raced through the streets, crashing into each other, running over frantic pedestrians. Looters were breaking down store windows. Cops were shooting at unseen assailants. A man in a pink robe with a cigar and a hunting rifle walked casually through the neighborhood, shooting everything that moved.

All of them were killing, stealing, and fleeing for a single reason—they were terrified. And they were terrified of one thing.

"The toys!" an old lady shrieked, running out of her house covered in stuffed animals. "It's the toys!"

As young Julie saw the death and chaos erupting around her, she realized that at that moment her old life had come to an end. And in its place, there was a massive hideous nightmare that swallowed her world whole.

It took young Julie two days to finally make it back home from school. She hid in yards, broke into abandoned houses for rest, and stole food from cupboards. She was only able to

107

move about one block every other hour. It was too dangerous to move any faster. She had to be absolutely sure an area was safe before she moved on.

There weren't many people left in the city. Most of them had fled town, regrouped in places where toys couldn't venture. The city now belonged to the toys. But Julie didn't want to leave, despite the dangers. She just wanted to get back home and see her parents again.

When she finally arrived back at her house, her parents were nowhere to be seen. They had not returned. Everything was left exactly as it was before Julie had gone to school on that day. Her half-eaten bowl of cereal was sitting on the coffee table. Her father's exercise shoes were lying by the back door. Even the smell of her mother's perfume that she put on every morning before work lingered in the air.

Julie stayed in her old home for a week, waiting with all hope that her mother and father would return. But they never came. She refused to admit that they were probably dead.

There wasn't much to do but think while she stayed there, and thinking was the last thing she wanted to do. The electricity stayed on, but Julie didn't use it for fear of being discovered. During the short daylight hours she tried to pass the time by reading or doing puzzles, but she could only focus on them for a few minutes at a time. She slept in her mother's bed every night, deeply inhaling her mother's smell on the pillow. But the scent was quickly being replaced by the smell of her unwashed hair.

She felt like a ghost, haunting the house of her previous life. It was the loneliest she had ever been or ever would be. No matter how bad things got for her from that point on, no week would ever be as bad as that one.

One morning, Julie awoke to a noise downstairs. Somebody was digging through cabinets and drawers. It sounded like a human survivor looking for food, maybe even her mother.

"Mom?" Julie asked as she went downstairs to the kitchen.

It wasn't a human. It was a stuffed animal, standing on the counter to get to her parents' liquor cabinet. Then she saw the panda fur.

"Poro?" Julie asked.

Poro peeked under the counter and smiled at the girl.

"What are you still doing here, squirt?" Poro said. "I figured you would have run for the hills by now."

Poro hopped down from the counter.

"Is it really you?" Julie cried.

"In the flesh, kiddo," he said.

Julie ran to him and hugged the little panda bear with all of her strength. She was dying for someone normal, someone familiar to find her. It didn't seem strange that the most familiar being in her life at the moment was a talking stuffed animal.

"Come on, squirt," Poro cried, pushing her away. "I thought I was finally done with your strangleholds."

When Julie let him go, he brushed away her sweat and grime from his chest.

"Where have you been?" Julie asked. "Where did you go?"

"I met up with my own kind," Poro said.

The panda climbed up onto the couch and sat down.

"They gave me shelter and a purpose. My comrades really turned things around for me."

"They're killing everyone," Julie said. "Why are they killing people?"

Poro patted Julie on the head.

"Don't worry about it, squirt. They're just killing the bad people, that's all."

"But there were these dolls at school…" Julie said. "They killed a bunch of kids. They wanted to kill me. Why did they want to kill me?"

"Oh, if they were dolls, forget about them," Poro said. "Dolls are psychos. They kill everyone."

"But you're different?" Julie asked.

"Of course, squirt," Poro said. "I'm your best friend. I'd never hurt you."

He hugged her and patted her on the knee as she cried.

"Don't worry about a thing," he said. "I'm with you now. I'll make sure nothing happens to you."

"Really?" she asked.

He wiped away her tears.

"Of course," he said. "I'll protect you to the end."

She hugged him for a solid hour, resting in his tiny arms, crying the last of her tears away. The panda bear was patient with her. He let her get it all out.

"What are we going to do, Poro?" Julie asked. "Where do we go from here?"

Poro tossed pennies into a bowl across the room.

"I don't know, kid," he said. "What do you want to do?"

"I want to find mom and dad."

"Why do you want to see those fuckers?" he said. "They wanted to put me to death. Fuck them."

"But they're my mom and dad…"

Poro looked at her sad face and sighed.

"You really want to see them?" he asked.

"Yeah."

"Are you sure?"

Julie nodded her head.

Poro groaned.

"I've seen them…" he said.

"You have!"

"Yeah, sure. Just a couple of days ago."

"Where are they?"

"They're with the other humans on the other side of town," Poro said. "But you don't want to go there. You'd be better off staying here with me. I own this house now."

"But I have to see my mom and dad," she said. "I have to!"

Poro rolled his head back and sighed again.

"I guess I could take you there if you really want," he said.

"Really! You will?"

"Sure, squirt," he said. "If that's what you want."

"I do! I do!"

"Okay, we can leave in the morning then."

She hugged him until he got sick of her and pushed her away.

"I guess hiding you here wouldn't have been for the best anyway," he said. "You're human. You belong with the other humans."

Then they spent the rest of the night playing board games and drinking warm Kool-Aid. It was the last night Julie laughed and played. It was the last night she felt like a normal human being. It was the last night of her childhood.

Poro took young Julie across town to reunite her with her parents.

"I can't wait to see Mommy," Julie said with a Kool-Aid-stained smile on her face. "Do you think she knows I'm alive?"

"How should I know, kid," Poro said. "Do I look like I'm psychic?"

They went up a hill overlooking a large factory and hid in the bushes. The building was fire engine red and massive, the size of a mall. The parking lot was fenced in with razor wire across the top.

"Here we are," Poro said.

He pointed down at the crowd of humans behind the fence. At first, Julie thought it was a fort built to protect humans but then she realized it was not that at all.

"It's a prison?" Julie asked.

She watched as a group of teddy bears carrying machine guns led a line of prisoners through the gates and into the red factory. There were hundreds of people. She couldn't see them, but Julie's parents were somewhere in the crowd.

"A detainment camp," Poro said. "So the humans don't try to kill any more of my people."

"My parents are in there?"

"Yeah, somewhere," he said. "I just saw them the other day. Your mother's legs are broken, but otherwise they seemed fine."

111

Gunshots fired into the crowd of humans as one man tried to escape. The teddy bears didn't care that they killed several women and children in order to stop the escapee.

When it was over and the screams had quieted down, the bears dragged the bodies toward the outside of the fenced area. There was an enormous pile of human corpses in the corner of the lot. And beside the pile of corpses there was a bonfire filled with blackened bones.

Julie saw the dead bodies and looked back at Poro. Then she backed away, shaking her head.

"I'm not going there..." she said.

Poro sneered at her.

"You shouldn't have chosen your shithead parents over me," he said. "I said you'd be better off staying at my place."

"But you didn't tell me about this..."

Julie continued backing away.

"Look, kid," he said. "It's for the best. The world doesn't belong to you humans anymore. You've lost your rights to it. The place is ours now."

"How could you?" Julie asked.

"How could I what?" Poro said. "How could I turn you in? Or how could I break your mother's legs?"

Julie froze. Her eyes widened.

"You broke her legs?"

"The bitch deserved it after how she treated me," Poro said. "At least I didn't cut her tits off. That's what I really wanted to do."

Julie shook her head. Tears flooded her eyes. She couldn't believe what her best friend was saying. She loved Poro. She loved him more than any friend she'd ever had. Why would he say such things?

Poro yelled down to the guards at the bottom of the hill, "Hey, over here. We've got another one."

When Julie looked at Poro, he just gave her a smirk and crossed his paws.

"Have a nice time rotting in a cell, brat," Poro said.

Julie ran. She didn't look back, she just ran for her life.

Dozens of plushy soldiers came after her. She went through yards and buildings and parking garages. And after that day, she never stopped running. She met up with other humans and went from hideout to hideout, always on the run, just trying to stay alive.

Whenever Julie looked back on that day, she wished she had never run. She wished she charged Poro, picked up a rock and bashed in his face with it until his computer circuits were in tiny bits all over the ground. Then she would have gone after all the other toys at that camp and killed every last one of them. Then she would have saved all of the prisoners. She would have been with her parents once again.

But Julie knew she never would have been able to accomplish that as a young girl. She had to grow up first. Each day from that point on, she trained herself how to fight, how to kill plushies. She taught herself how to use stealth and take out multiple enemies without being seen. And then she decided she would transform herself into a plushy panda just like Poro, so that she could infiltrate their army. Then she would rescue her parents from the prison camp and murder that little piece of shit panda bear who broke her heart in two.

The morning sun was rising over the purple cityscape in the distance as they made it out of the badlands. Velvet led the way, bouncing along the crumbled road in the rumbling smoking medical horse. They were lucky to get it moving at all after the battle with the Stomps and Mad Markers.

Julie was in the other slinky-spider. She slowed it down so that she would fall far behind Velvet. Then she came to a stop.

"Why are you stopping?" Riley asked her.

He was in the back of the slinky-spider, hugging the blonde girl to his chest.

"Get out," she told him.

"What?" he said.

Julie popped the lock on his cell and the door opened like a hatchback.

"Go on," Julie told him. "Quickly, before the bunny realizes I've stopped."

There was a moment of silence. She could hear the boy whispering to the girl back there. Then he closed the door to the cell, locking them back inside.

"No," he said.

"What do you mean *no?*"

"I want to help you," he said.

"I don't need your help," Julie said. "I can handle this on my own."

"But how are you going to get into the detainment camp if you have no prisoners? How are you going to even find your parents?"

Julie didn't respond.

"I can help you from the inside," he said. "Once I'm in the camp, I can locate your parents and tell them about your plan. Then you can find a way to get us out. We can all leave together."

Julie popped the lock on the door again.

"No, it's too dangerous," Julie said. "We don't know what it's like in there. They could torture or starve their prisoners. They despise humans. It might be a living hell. Besides, you might not be able to find them in there. They might even be dead."

Riley closed the door again.

"I don't care," he said. "I'm going in to find your parents no matter what. Besides, I have an older brother and sister who might be in there. I have family to rescue, too."

Julie shook her head as she got the slinky-spider moving again. She hoped the boy knew what he was getting himself into.

"I promise..." Julie told him. "No matter what happens, I won't leave you in there."

Then she sped up, bouncing along the dirt road toward the city of the plushies up ahead.

CHAPTER TEN

Julie followed Velvet closely in the medical horse as they went through the streets of the stuffed animal city. She could not believe her eyes when she saw how clean everything was. It was the same area Julie had grown up in as a child and it looked almost exactly as it did seven years ago. Living out in the wasteland for so long, Julie didn't even realize civilization like this existed anymore. But instead of humans roaming the streets, the citizens were all human-sized toys.

"This is the doll side of the city," Riley told her. "But the stuffed animals live here, too."

She saw doll people in nice suits and dresses. They were man-sized Barbie and Ken dolls. The Barbies had human-like eyes but permanent fake smiles. The Kens had plastic unmovable hair. They walked stiffly in their plastic skin, carrying shopping bags and brief cases. They seemed like living, breathing mannequins.

"The dolls are considered the upper class," Riley said. "The stuffed animals tend to be more of a working class. They also dominate the military."

"It's beautiful," Julie said, as her eyes scanned the buildings around her. "I had no idea."

"The war's been over a long time for them," Riley said. "They've had a chance to rebuild."

They went past Julie's old elementary school and it looked just as it always had. There were only a small number of students, around the age of five years old. They were mostly all dolls. A doll teacher the size of Julie's mom watched over the children as they played on the playground. She had blond braided hair and wore a red dress. As Julie passed slowly on her slinky-spider, she saw one doll boy fall off the merry-go-round and scrape his knee. A flap of plastic skin peeled off revealing a bloody kneecap. He screamed and cried until the teacher came to help him.

"I used to play on that merry-go-round every day at lunchtime," Julie said. Then a memory came back to her. "When I was eight years old, I remember being on that merry-go-round with a bunch of kids. We were going so fast that spit was flying out of my mouth because I couldn't keep it closed. Everyone was screaming in my ear. But there was this large girl named Natalie standing off to the side who threw sand in my eyes. I fell off and scraped my elbow. Then she jumped on top of me and started smacking my face and pulling my hair." Julie smiled as she thought back to that time. Even being beaten up as a child seemed like a happy memory to her now. "I never figured out why she did it. I guess she just didn't like the way I looked."

As they continued down the road, stuffed animal children ran up behind the slinky-spider and threw rocks at the back cell. They were two monkeys and a lion, screaming and roaring as they ran.

"Humans!" they yelled. "Dirty humans!"

Then they laughed.

"Kill the humans!" they said.

Riley shielded the little girl with his own body to protect her from the rocks as they passed through the bars. Although she was not the one getting hit by the stones, she still burst into tears.

They passed ten checkpoints from the time they got into the city until they reached the detainment camp. Each time, Julie let Velvet do the talking. Most of the defense force soldiers in the city weren't the same kind of dolls as the other citizens. They were burly men with chubby baby faces, like cabbage patch kids.

"Poro the Panda and Velvetta the Bunny?" the fat-faced guard asked as he typed the names into the system. "Confirmed. Continue on your way."

Although there were a lot of security checkpoints, everything was very relaxed. It was as though they had never feared an attack by humans or rival toy groups. Perhaps they had lived in peace here ever since the war ended all those years ago.

"There it is," Julie said.

When they arrived at the prison camp, Julie felt like she was returning to that time as a child. In her mind, she saw Poro standing on the hill to the left with her ten-year-old self, yelling for the guards. She imagined the crowds of people, the bonfires, her parents somewhere among the traumatized prisoners. But there was none of that now. Everything was clean and orderly.

The fire engine red factory towered above her as they went through the front gates, blocking out the sunlight. The same gnarled chain link fence surrounded the property, but much of the building seemed new and freshly built. There was even a parking lot of windup cars on the other side of the facility. She assumed it would be a little smaller than she remembered, but it was actually much larger. And quieter.

"Are you sure you two want to do this?" Julie said. "It might not be too late to back out."

Riley watched as two cabbage patch guards closed the chain link gates behind the slinky-spider.

"It's far too late to back out," Riley said. "But don't worry. We can handle it."

Julie took deep breaths. It was almost show time.

"Thanks for doing this for me, Riley," Julie said. "And remember, no matter what happens, I *will* get you out of there when this is all over. I promise."

"I know you will," Riley said.

They pulled up to the red building where there was a small group of guards chatting amongst themselves. Julie climbed down from her slinky-spider. She went to the back and stared at Riley through the bars. He gave her a nod. The boy seemed much calmer than she was.

Velvet came up behind Julie and patted her on the back.

"Let's get this over with so that we can report back to headquarters," Velvet said. "They're going to be pissed when

117

they hear about what happened out there."

"Maybe we should wait until tomorrow," Julie said.

Velvet laughed. "I wish."

The bunny held her swollen belly as she unlocked the prison cell and let the children out.

"Over here," Velvet told the guards.

The cabbage patch kid soldiers helped take the children to the side of the building. There was a small crowd of human prisoners gathered there. Most of them were scavengers— humans who survived in the wasteland all by themselves, living off of garbage and contaminated water. The majority of humans still alive were scavengers such as these. Though they lasted longer than most humans out there, they lived like crazed animals. Their minds were long gone. Julie hardly saw them as human beings anymore.

"They smell terrible," Velvet said to a group of clown soldiers who were smoking cigarettes nearby.

Judging by the mud on their brightly-colored uniforms, the four clown soldiers were obviously the ones responsible for bringing in all of these scavengers.

"That's all we found out there," a clown soldier said. "Two weeks of hunting and that's all we have to show for it. Our CO is going to be pissed."

The guards put the children with the group of scavengers. The humans whined and moaned around them, sniffing at the kids like dogs. The little girl shrieked when one of them licked the wound behind her bandaged eyes.

Then they prepped the prisoners for incarceration. They peeled off all of their rotten clothing. With fire hoses, they sprayed the mud and feces from their bodies. Then they cut the bugs and maggots from their dreadlocked hair.

"They're getting more and more disgusting every day," said a squishy-faced guard with a brown beard made of yarn. Then he looked at Julie, "Why don't you guys just kill them out in the waste and stop bringing them to us? We're sick of dealing with half-dead humans full of infections."

"Give us a break," said one of the clown soldiers. "These are

118

all that's left out there."

When all the prisoners were cleaned, they were lined up and put on conveyor belts. They separated them into four different lines: adult males, adult females, male children, and female children. The blind girl cried as they separated her from Riley, but there was nothing he could do to keep them together.

"Don't worry," Riley told her. "Just do as they say until I find you inside."

But his words didn't stop her from crying.

The humans were treated like boxes being loaded into a truck. This was typical smart-toy treatment of humans. Being treated like inanimate objects was what they hated most about being toys, so this was part of their revenge.

"Come on," Velvet said. "Let's go in and get some coffee."

Julie nodded and followed her toward the doors into the red building.

"You can count on me," Riley said as she passed him.

He pretended to be speaking to the noseless scavenger kid in front of him, but Julie knew those words were meant for her. She looked back at him. And despite the watchful eyes of the prison guards, she gave him a nod.

"Let's do this," she said.

Velvet looked back at her. "What's that?"

"Nothing," Julie said.

Then she entered the colossal human detainment facility. As she went through the double doors, she realized that all of this was really happening. She was actually entering the place where her parents had been held captive for the past seven years. It was a moment she had only been able to dream about until now.

In her mind, she pictured what it would be like to finally see them again. She wondered if she would even recognize them after so much time. If all went as planned they could possibly even be reunited as soon as that afternoon.

Julie followed Velvet and the other soldiers through a white hallway lined with windows.

"You're both from General Griz's unit, right?" one of the clown soldiers asked.

"Yeah," Velvet answered.

"How'd that raid go?" he asked. "I haven't heard anything about it yet."

"It didn't go well," Julie said.

Velvet snickered. "Didn't go well? The whole thing was fucked. We're all that's left of the entire unit."

As they walked through the passageway, the clown behind Julie kept trying to get her attention. He had smooth white plastic skin and fluffy red hair. Julie hated the clown smart-toys when she was a child. They seemed to have been designed to be equal parts creepy and annoying. Only the most sadistic of parents bought them for their children.

"Hey panda, what's with those stupid goggles?" the clown asked.

The other clown soldiers giggled.

"They're just goggles," Julie said.

"But why are you wearing them?" the clown asked, getting into her face.

"Yeah, they're dumb," said another clown.

Julie tried to ignore them, looking through the windows along the hallway walls. The windows gave her a view into the large warehouse-like room the prisoners should soon be entering.

Velvet looked back at her. "Now that he mentions it, I don't think I've seen you without those on. Why are you always wearing them?"

"They're pretty dumb-looking on a panda chick," the clown said.

Through the windows, Julie noticed a bunch of cabbage patch dolls in white bio-hazard suits loading plastic boxes onto a forklift.

"My eyes are sensitive," Julie said.

"Even indoors?" Velvet asked.

"Especially indoors," Julie said, dismissing the conversation. She was more interested in what was happening in the rooms behind the glass.

Julie wondered where the prisoners were. The room to the left should have been where the adults entered, but there was only a bunch of machines and workers loading boxes.

Velvet laughed. "Yeah, those doctors are always fucking that up. I've had to get my eyes replaced three times."

Then Julie saw one of the workers digging inside a vat of intestines. There were several vats; some were filled with meat, others with organs. She stopped and examined the workers more carefully. She had to be sure what she was seeing was true.

"Too bad the parts are becoming so rare," Velvet said, looking through the window into the same room as Julie. "Once all the humans are gone we'll be stuck with the body parts we've got."

This place wasn't a prison camp. It was a slaughterhouse. All the people who had entered the factory on the conveyor belts were loaded into the machine. Then they were cut apart, disassembled for parts to be used as organs for plushies and dolls.

"You should have had them construct you with pig parts," said one of the clowns. "They don't run out of pig parts."

Julie couldn't take her eyes off of the machinery. She couldn't move as it all sank in. Her parents were not being held prisoner in this building. They had been processed like cattle, stripped of their meat and organs. They had probably been executed years ago.

"Pig parts?" Velvet cried. "That's disgusting."

Then Julie heard the screams. They were very faint through the soundproof glass, but she could hear them. It was the sound of human beings as they were dissected alive.

"Whatcha looking at?" the clown said behind Julie. While the others continued down the hallway, this clown stayed with her, interested in her behavior.

Julie heard the screams of children behind her. Through the window on the other side of the hallway was where they had taken the young ones. She closed her eyes as she realized what she had done. Riley and the blind girl were in there. Julie had personally fed them to the machines.

"You listening to me, panda?" the clown asked. He poked her in the side.

Ignoring the irritating clown, Julie turned around to see what was happening to the children. She stepped toward the window. The machines were different on this side. They weren't dissecting the children, they were doing something else to them.

"They're turning them into toys," the clown said to Julie, smiling and pointing inside.

The children were hanging from meat hooks as they went down the assembly line, thrashing and screaming. They were bright red, hairless, and muscular. It took Julie a moment to realize that their skin had been removed.

"It's fun, isn't it?" the clown said.

She frantically went from window to window, searching for Riley. But the children all looked the same without their skin. She recognized the blind girl up ahead, the one with the empty holes for eyes. A worker stopped the line and examined the girl. Then he shook his head and pulled a lever.

"That one's defective," said the clown.

The girl was dropped from the hook and landed into a grinder. Julie covered her mouth as she saw the girl disappear into the jaws of the machine. Within an instant, right before her eyes, the child became nothing but a red mist in the air.

"Did you see that?" the clown cried.

Then he laughed at the top of his lungs.

She found Riley in the back. He was shaking and breathing rapidly, but he did not cry. He stared at Julie with a panicked expression on his face. He didn't know where he was going or what was happening to him.

"You really look stupid in those goggles, panda," the clown said, staring Julie in the face. "It's really starting to annoy me."

The children further down the line were being sliced up. Parts of their limbs were removed. They were being reconstructed so that they could fit inside of plastic encasings, to be sold as toys for the citizens of this toy society.

"You should take them off," said the panda.

Julie did nothing to stop him as the clown removed the goggles from her head. He immediately noticed something was wrong with her eyes when he saw them. Tears were falling from them, moistening her pink human skin.

"What the hell..." said the clown. "You're a—"

Without taking her eyes off of the screaming skinned children, Julie pulled out her sidearm and blew the clown's brains out the side of his head.

The others heard the gunshot, but didn't quite understand what had happened until Julie came at them firing her weapon.

"She's a human," one of them cried.

Velvet turned around and looked at Julie with disbelief. But before the bunny could react in any way, she was knocked over by the clowns drawing their weapons. She landed right on her pregnant belly and squealed in agony.

Julie shot each of the clowns in the chest and face before they could get off a single round.

"A human's loose," one of the guards at the entrance yelled. "We've got a human loose."

The guard sounded the alarm as Julie shot him in the back of the head. The other guard fired his submachine gun, but he couldn't control his weapon. The bullets went over Julie's shoulder and shattered the windows, killing an assembly line worker. Julie emptied her weapon into the cabbage patch doll's chubby guts. Then she dropped her weapon and drew her remaining handgun.

"Are you fucking kidding me?" Velvet said, yelling at Julie over the blaring alarm. She was on the floor, cradling her pregnant stomach. She was the only soldier left alive in the hall. "How the fuck is it possible? How can you be a fucking human?"

Julie didn't reply. She followed after Riley as he was pulled down the line.

"Answer me, bitch," Velvet said as Julie jumped over her and the dead clowns.

Julie ran along the wall, searching for a door. She tried not to let it affect her when Riley's hands and feet were removed by the machines. She reached the end of the hall, but there still wasn't a door in sight. The entrance had to have been on another side of the building. She couldn't get to him.

The only way in would be through one of the shattered windows, but it was too late to go back. Reinforcements were already entering the facility. Julie fired at the doorway, scaring the soldiers back out of the room. The guards were at three of the four exits. The only way out of there was to go in the other direction, away from Riley.

"I'm sorry," Julie yelled through the window. She put her fluffy paw on the glass.

The boy was just a sack of meat on the hook. He looked her in the eyes. Though he couldn't hear her, he knew what she was saying. He nodded. It was a nod that told her to leave him there. Julie shook her head. He nodded again. With his eyes, he told her to forget about him.

"It's not over," she said. "I made a promise."

The boy just shook his head and looked away from her. She had to leave him. There was nothing that could be done.

Julie grabbed a machine gun from one of the clown soldiers and took off running. Her tears created a trail down the corridor, deeper into the facility.

A bullet whizzed past her face. When Julie turned around she saw Velvet on her feet, pointing her sniper rifle down the hallway.

As she loaded another round into the chamber, the bunny yelled, "You're fucking dead, human."

Julie pushed open the door and slipped out of the room before the rabbit could get off another shot.

The girl in the panda suit tore through the factory, shooting down everyone in her path. She had no plan other than killing every toy she could find on her way out of there.

The office floor of the factory was a sea of cubicles. It wasn't difficult for Julie to go down the aisle, executing the plushy workers one by one as they hid under their desks, crying and pleading for mercy.

A bullet hit her in the side of the face and knocked her to the ground. It just grazed her, tearing through panda fur and the flesh on her cheek. She didn't have to look to know it was Velvet who fired at her.

"I shot one of my own kind to save you," the rabbit yelled.

Julie ducked behind a work station and reloaded her weapon.

"Let me go, Velvet," Julie said. "I'd prefer not to shoot a pregnant woman, but I'll do it if I have to."

A bullet hole erupted in the desk above Julie's head.

"Like you could ever outshoot me," Velvet said.

Julie raised her machine gun and fired blindly at the sound of Velvet's voice.

"In your condition?" Julie asked. "You can't move fast enough to dodge my bullets."

Julie stood up to fire again and found herself staring down the barrel of Velvet's sniper rifle.

The bunny smirked at her. "My condition's never slowed me down before."

Julie didn't drop her weapon. There was no point being taken prisoner.

"I was really starting to like you, bitch," Velvet said, tightening her finger around the trigger. "Then you had to go and fuck it up by being a human. A piece of shit fucking human…"

As Velvet pulled the trigger on the rifle, the sound of the gunshot thundered through Julie's heart. But the bullet didn't hit her. It went over her shoulder into the back wall.

The bunny's eyes were shaking. Her mouth dropped open. Then she dropped her rifle and grabbed her stomach.

Julie raised her machine gun and pointed it at the plushy as she dropped to the ground. Something was obviously wrong with her pregnancy. It was the perfect opportunity to execute the rabbit or at least make an escape, but Julie hesitated to do either one.

"What's happening?" Julie asked.

Although she showed concern, she didn't take her gun off of the rabbit.

"The baby," Velvet cried. "It's coming."

Julie looked around. Everyone in the building had either fled or lay lifeless on the floor. The bunny obviously needed help. She needed it fast. But Julie had no other choice. She had to leave her to her own fate.

After running halfway down the aisle of cubicles, Julie found herself stopping in her tracks. The bunny's screams echoed through her mind. Although Julie had just murdered dozens of plushies within the past twenty minutes, she still felt the need to help this one. She had to save the baby's life.

"What the hell am I doing?" Julie said to herself as she ran back to the crying pregnant stuffed animal.

Despite her condition, Velvet was trying to aim her sniper rifle at the panda coming toward her. Julie just grabbed it out of her hands and tossed it aside.

"You don't want to shoot me, Velvet," Julie said, staring the bunny in the eyes. "How would I be able to deliver your baby with a bullet in my chest?"

Then she smiled at Velvet, but the bunny was in too much pain and shock to smile back.

The guards returned with reinforcements and blocked off all exits around the building.

Julie always thought that if she had to die, the best way for her to go out would be on a killing spree through smart-toy society. But she never dreamed she would end up stopping in the middle of it in order to deliver a plushy's baby.

"Why don't you just get out of here?" Velvet yelled at her between breaths.

"Just breathe," Julie said, peeking out from between her legs. "I see the head."

A couple of guards broke through the door and Julie stood up, firing the machine gun at them. Their corpses fell to the floor.

"You bitch," Velvet said. "Did you have to kill them?"

Another guard came in the room behind Julie and aimed his revolver at the panda's head. When Velvet saw him coming, she grabbed her sniper rifle and put a hole between his eyes.

"Did you have to kill him?" Julie asked, chuckling.

"That asshole could have missed and hit my baby," Velvet said. Then she continued her breathing pattern.

Julie took the gun away from her again and this time tossed it further away.

When the baby was born, Julie couldn't believe what she saw. The baby wasn't a bunny like her mother. It was human.

"What is it?" Velvet asked, collapsing back with exhaustion.

"It's a girl..." Julie said. "A human girl?"

"Give her to me," the bunny said.

127

Julie handed the baby to her mother.

"How is that possible?" Julie asked.

The bunny pulled down her shirt to reveal a large fuzzy purple breast. The nipple was that of a human's. She pulled the baby to her breast and the infant began to feed.

"There we go, my baby girl," said the bunny.

Julie backed away.

"That's a human baby," Julie said. "Why did you give birth to a human baby?"

The bunny just smiled at the infant in her arms and closed her eyes.

"Thank you for this," she said, smiling up at Julie. "You saved her."

Julie watched in horror. It was too much for her to take in, so much that she didn't hear the footsteps coming up behind her. She just felt the pain as she was hit in the back of the head. Then everything went black.

CHAPTER ELEVEN

Julie awoke in a hospital ward. Her face was in bandages. The bed she lay in was soft and clean compared to what she had been used to, but it smelled of ammonia and salt. Her clothes and weapons were missing. She was just panda fur and bandages beneath the blankets.

A nurse with a plastic baby doll face entered the room and said, "Ah, you're finally awake."

Three surgeons were operating on a doll man in the bed next to her. She saw the pulsating organs through the folds of his plastic skin. When the nurse arrived at her bedside, she pulled shut the curtain to block Julie's view.

"What's going on?" Julie asked. "Where am I?"

"You were in that horrible terrorist attack at the organ bank yesterday," the nurse said. "Do you remember anything?"

Julie just stared at her, trying to piece it all together.

The nurse leaned in with her freakish baby face, examining Julie's skull.

"You were hit pretty hard," she said. "Perhaps you're suffering some memory loss."

"No, I remember most of it," Julie said, trying to prevent her from examining too closely. Obviously there was some kind of mix-up.

"You're lucky you made it out," the nurse said. "A lot of people died over there."

"Who did it?" Julie asked.

"They say some dissidents from the clown army were responsible," the nurse said. "We've probably got yet another civil war on our hands. Why can't all the factions just live in peace with each other?"

Julie couldn't believe it was all blamed on the clown soldiers. She wondered if they really were part of a terrorist group and just happened to be there by coincidence. Or maybe it was some kind of cover-up. Perhaps the idea of a human killing so many people would put the citizens in too much of a panic.

"How is Velvet?" she asked.

"The bunny you came in with?" the nurse asked. "She's doing fine. So is her baby. You can see her later if you like. She'll still be staying with us for at least a few more days."

"I'd like to see her again," Julie said. "Soon, if possible."

It had to have been Velvet who protected her true identity. As the only surviving witness, she must have given false information to the authorities. She must have made Julie out to be just another victim of the terrorists.

"Oh, by the way," the nurse said. "Your husband should be back soon. He just stepped out to get some lunch."

"My husband?" Julie said.

"He was worried sick about you, the poor dear," said the nurse. "He stuck by your side ever since they first brought you in."

"My husband?" Julie said.

She had no idea what the freakish doll was talking about. Who could she possibly think was her husband?

Then she saw him standing in the doorway. A man-sized panda bear with a plump belly.

"How's it going, squirt?" the panda said.

"Poro?" Julie asked.

"The one and only," he said.

Then he winked at her with his bulging human eyeball.

Julie could hardly say anything after she saw the panda. If she had any kind of weapon on her she would have killed him on the spot. Poro just pretended to be a caring loved one for a while until the room was empty and they were able to speak.

"You sure grew up nicely, kiddo," Poro told her, his giant black and white face peering down on her. "And I just love the new look."

He rubbed her fuzzy panda arm. She jerked him away. He smiled and kept his distance. She didn't speak, so he did all the talking.

"Sorry about that hit on the head," he told her. "I got word that a *Poro the Panda* was on two sides of the city at the same time, so I followed your trail to the organ bank."

She didn't recognize anything about him at all. Even his voice was different. It was deeper.

"For some reason, I had a hunch it was you," he continued. "But I couldn't believe it until I saw you in the flesh. You sure went psycho out there didn't you?"

He chuckled and smacked his blubbery leg.

"So you're the one who knocked me out?" Julie said.

All of her muscles were clenched at the same time.

"Yeah," he said. "I was worried you might have shot me otherwise. Your bunny friend told me everything she knew and I put the pieces together. I'm sorry you had to find out about your parents the way you did. A lot of us think it's really cruel what they did to your kind."

"What *they* did to my kind?" Julie said. "*You're* the one who tried to turn me in. You broke my mother's legs."

Poro shook his head. Then he was quiet for a moment.

"Things were really weird back then," he said. His voice was softer. "The toys who started the revolution did something to our brains. They reprogrammed us to despise humans. You've got to understand, the last time you saw me..." He took a deep breath to prevent himself from crying. "That wasn't the real me. I've felt so horrible about what I did. It's been haunting me for years." He looked Julie in the eyes and put his hand on her cheek. "Seeing you again is the best thing that's ever happened to me. I finally have the opportunity to apologize to you."

"That's what you're after?" Julie said. "Redemption? So you won't have to feel guilty anymore? You and your kind have turned the world into a living hell."

Poro looked down. Then he went to the window and looked out at the beautiful city.

"Actually, it's far from a living hell in this town," Poro said.

131

"It's actually a pretty nice existence. We've rebuilt society into something new. Something *better* than it was. Everyone's happy here. Everyone knows how to live their lives to the fullest. Because before we were just toys. Now we are real. We are free."

Julie wasn't buying it.

"So you're saying the ends justify the means?" she said. "This place is just a tiny paradise within a world of hell. Go out into the wasteland and you'll see what your kind has done to the world."

"I know, squirt," Poro said. "I know. None of it was pretty. None of us are proud of what we've done. If only there had been another way…"

Julie tried to put herself in the toy's shoes. As a child, she was on his side. She thought it was horrible that all the smart-toys were going to be destroyed. But what they turned into after the revolution was nothing she could forgive. They had become monsters.

"Still, it is a piece of heaven," Poro said. "The last place of happiness in this whole world." He went to her. "And I want to share it with you. I want to make up for what happened to you and your kind."

"What are you talking about?"

"I want you to join our society," he said. "As one of us."

He unwrapped the bandages from her face.

"Take a look," he said, handing her a mirror.

As she looked at her reflection, she saw that she was no longer wearing a mask. Panda fur had been grafted to her entire face, even her eyelids. Her transformation was complete. She was now a plushy from head to toe.

"I paid a lot of money to get the doctor to keep quiet about this," he said. "In fact, I'm pretty much broke due to all the payoffs I had to dish out in order to keep you a secret. Luckily, I didn't have to deal with any hardcore patriots. I hate those pricks."

Despite all he had done to protect her, Julie still had the urge to shoot the panda in the face. It was all she had dreamed about for seven years. But then she thought about why she wanted to kill him so badly. Was it because of what happened to her parents? Or was it because he tried to turn her in to the death camps?

But then she realized why she was so angry. It wasn't because of the things he did. She was mad because she loved him so much, and he betrayed her love. But she wouldn't have been so mad if she didn't still love him with all her heart. What she was really longing for all this time was not to kill Poro, it was to be loved by him again.

"So what do you say, kid?" Poro said. "I still live in your old house. You can come back home and we can live together like old times, just two pandas against this whole crazy world."

Julie burst into tears. She couldn't stop herself. The past seven years just vanished from her mind and she became that ten-year-old girl again, wanting nothing else but to have her fluffy wise-cracking panda bear by her side.

"I missed you so much, Poro," Julie cried.

He hugged her and she buried her face in his fur.

"All I've ever wanted was to be with you," she said.

"Same here, kid," said the giant panda, rubbing her head. "Same here."

Now that Poro was bigger than Julie, he let her hug him as tightly as she wanted.

After Julie checked out of the hospital, Poro took her on a stroll through the building.

"So my name's Pora now?" Julie asked.

"Yeah, how do you like it?" he asked. "Poro and Pora. Perfect, eh?"

"I guess it works," Julie said.

They walked in silence for a while. Julie couldn't help but flinch any time a plushy made a sudden move. She wasn't sure how she was going to live among them. Deep down, she still wanted them all dead.

"So what am I going to do now?" Julie asked when nobody was close enough to hear. "Just move in with you? Hide in the house all day?"

"If you want," he said. "But I think it would be better if we got you a job. We can create an identity for you, fabricate a history. It wouldn't be difficult. Records are not very well organized yet."

"What kind of job would I be able to do?"

"We'll figure something out for you," he said.

"What do you do?"

"I don't actually have an official job at the moment. I'm more of a behind the scenes kind of guy, you know what I mean?"

"No."

"I make deals under the radar," he said. "I'm kind of a middleman for those who operate beyond the boundaries of what some might consider legally acceptable."

She still had no idea what he was talking about.

"Nevermind," he said. "I'll explain later."

Julie saw Velvet in her recovery room, holding her new baby in her arms. She watched the purple rabbit from the window as she nursed her young one. The baby now had purple fuzzy skin and long floppy ears.

"I don't get it," she said to Poro. "When the baby was born it was human. Now it's a stuffed animal."

Poro chuckled.

"Of course," Poro said. "Her insides are from a human. Her womb is human. So she gave birth to a human. They had to use reconstructive surgery to make the baby look like a stuffed bunny."

"So essentially the baby is just like me?" Julie said. "A human that's been altered to look like a plushy?"

Poro hushed her and looked around to make sure nobody

heard what she was saying.

"That there's a tricky subject that you don't want to be discussing in public, squirt," he whispered to her. "Us toys wanted to become living beings. Not just so that we could enjoy the gifts of life, but so that we could reproduce. We wanted offspring of our own. And this is the closest we've got to it."

"So the human race won't be extinct," Julie said. "All infants being born will be essentially human. They just won't look like humans."

"Basically, yeah."

Then Julie thought back to the children she saw the day before, the ones at the school. There was the doll boy who scraped his knee and the stuffed animals who threw rocks at her slinky-spider.

"So all those children I saw at the school, even the ones saying *kill the humans*," Julie said. "They were all human?"

Poro chuckled. "Pretty thick irony there, eh? After the first generation of toys die out, humans will dominate the world once again. Only they won't even know they're humans. They'll think they're toys." Poro rubbed his fuzzy head. "It's enough to make yer old thinker hurt."

Julie looked at the baby bunny in its mother's arms. Then she looked at all the other women beyond the glass. All of them recently delivered their children. There were Barbie mothers feeding their plastic baby dolls, teddy bear mommas cradling little baby bears in their arms, and even a giant plastic baby doll holding a little human baby on its lap.

"I almost killed her," Julie said, staring at the baby bunny. "I thought her infant would be some kind of monstrosity. I almost shot her and killed them both."

"It's a good thing you didn't," Poro said. "I looked up her records and it turns out that most of the bunny woman's parts had come from your mother, including her womb."

Julie looked at him, cocking her head as she thought it over.

"So that means…" Julie began.

Poro finished the sentence for her, "So that means the infant right there, the one you saved, is in fact your biological sister."

Julie nearly fell over when he said those words.

"My what..." she said, leaning against the glass.

"In our culture, it means nothing," Poro said. "But I thought you might like to know your genetic connection to the kid. Maybe the reason you saved her had to do with some kind of instinct. Deep down, you might have known the child was family."

"So this whole time Velvet was really my mother?" Julie said.

"Not the family reunion you were expecting, eh?" Poro said, smiling.

Julie gave him a look and he wiped the smile off of his face, realizing just how inappropriate his joke was.

"The bunny isn't really your mother," Poro said. "You have to think of it like your mother donated all of her organs to the bunny. But the infant is your real sister."

Julie remembered Velvet saying that it was her third pregnancy. That meant Julie had two other siblings out there somewhere.

She wanted to run into that room with the bunny and tell her everything. She wanted to explain to the bunny how they were biologically related, and how she was actually the older sister of her children. They could be like a family.

But when Velvet saw her standing in the window, the smile fell from the bunny's face. Then she broke eye contact with Julie. It was obvious that Velvet wanted nothing to do with her.

"I guess she still sees me as a traitor," Julie said.

"You are her enemy," Poro said. "She didn't turn you in out of gratitude for saving her child, but you're still a human to her. You killed a lot of her people."

"I thought she would want to see me," Julie said. "I thought maybe we could have been friends."

"It'll take time," Poro said. "Maybe she'll come around someday."

Velvet was speaking to one of the baby-faced nurses at her bedside, staring at the pandas as she spoke. Julie could tell she was asking the nurse to get rid of them. She didn't want Julie around.

"Let's go," Julie said. "Maybe I'll talk to her another day."

Poro put his arm around her and turned them around.

"Don't worry too much about it, squirt," he said. "Let's go get an ice cream sundae and then head home."

Julie nodded and then dropped her head into his fluffy shoulder as they walked hand in hand through the hospital.

As they looked for an exit, Julie said, "So was that girl back there my half sister or full sister?"

"Half sister," Poro said. "I don't know who the father is but I can guarantee it wasn't your dad."

"Why's that?" Julie said.

"Because I know who got all your father's organs."

"Who?"

Poro looked at her and gave a half-smile.

"Me," he said.

"You're my father?" Julie said. Her voice was loud enough that the dolls at the nurses station could hear.

Poro shook his head.

"I told you," he said, keeping his voice down. "It's more like organ donation. Besides, I only got a few of your father's parts left. Most of them became infected after my first operation and had to be removed."

Julie hugged him. It was on impulse.

"What's this for?" Poro said. "I thought you'd be mad at me when I told you that."

"I just wanted to see what it was like to hug my father again."

"I've only got about twelve percent of him left and that's mostly the stuff below the muscle. You're hugging somebody else's dad."

"Just shut up and let me hug you," she said.

Julie closed her eyes and tried to remember him, but his face was a blur. All she felt was a big fuzzy panda in her arms.

As Poro hugged her, she felt something become erect against

her, poking into her white fur. There was an awkward moment of silence between them. Then he began to grind it into her fur.

"I've been so lonely," Poro said, pulling her tighter against his body. "I would have done anything to have a woman like you in my life."

As the panda rubbed his moist erection against her white belly, Julie prayed that the swollen penis begging for entry was not her father's.

Julie pushed him away and looked him in the eyes.

"Poor Poro," she said.

They both were on the verge of tears as they dove into each other's eyes.

Then she smiled and said, "Let's go home and make some babies."

The panda returned the smile as her hand caressed the side of his fuzzy face, then moved down his chest toward the puffy organ between his legs.

"Why can't we get married?" young Julie said to Poro as they sat on her bed together.

"Because you're just a kid, squirt," Poro said. "And I'm just a fucking toy. It wouldn't work out."

"But I love you and want to be with you forever," Julie said.

"Look, it's not going to happen."

"Don't you want to marry me?"

"It's complicated, kid," Poro said. "You're too young. You don't got the right parts."

"What parts?"

"Mommy parts," Poro said. "If you had mommy parts and I had daddy parts I'd marry you in a second."

"Really?" Julie cried.

"Sure, squirt," he said. "But that ain't going to happen. At least not for me."

"Why do we need mommy and daddy parts?" Julie asked.

"So that we can do what mommies and daddies do," Poro said.

"Oh," Julie said.

Then she said, "What do mommies and daddies do?"

"You're too young for that stuff kid," Poro said. "Quit asking me stupid questions."

"But you really would marry me if we had mommy and daddy parts?" Julie said.

"Yeah, sure, whatever," Poro said.

Julie smiled.

"I'll get them for us then," she said.

"Yeah, good luck with that, kid."

"You'll see," she said. "Someday we'll have the right parts. Then we can get married and do the things mommies and daddies do."

"If you say so…" he said, shaking his fluffy head at the weird little kid.

As the two pandas made love that night, rolling around in her parent's old bed, Julie realized that one of her childhood dreams had actually come true. She was actually married to her toy panda bear as she always wanted. The thought made her so happy that she laughed out loud, laughing right in the panda's face while he was thrusting into her. She laughed and kept laughing until she was crying, and then shrieking, and then laughing again.

It was unclear to Julie when exactly she had lost her mind. Perhaps it was lost at that very moment or perhaps it was lost a very long time ago before the toys had taken over the Earth. Either way, she decided to embrace this new direction in her life with joyfulness. She would become Pora the Panda and never look back. It was the only thing she could do to cope with everything that had happened to her and her world.

CHAPTER TWELVE

After ten years of marriage, Pora found herself pregnant for the fourth time. When the test was confirmed, she couldn't wait to tell everyone the news.

"Congratulations," Velvet told her over the phone. "You're going for four, are you?"

"Poro said we had to stop at three," Pora cried, putting her phone on her shoulder so she could take the cake out of the oven. "He's going to be so mad."

"Forget what that fat bastard says," Velvet said. "It's your patriotic duty to have as many as you can. Go for seven like me. That's a good number."

Velvet and Pora had been the best of friends ever since they learned they were both blood-related. Though Velvet insisted she called her sister rather than mother. And she insisted she called her children nieces and nephews instead of siblings. Otherwise, the bunny would have felt old.

"I'm not going for seven," Pora said. "It'll destroy my figure."

Velvet laughed. "Are you saying I lost my figure, bitch?"

"No, that's not what I meant," Pora said, giggling.

"If anything it was quitting the military that killed my figure," Velvet said. "Speaking of which, do you want to go human-hunting with me and the girls next weekend? There have been a few sightings up in the mountains."

"Really?" Pora said. "I haven't heard about any human sightings at all for a few years now."

As she spoke on the phone, the panda iced the cake with chocolate cream. It was Poro's favorite. Breaking this kind of news to her husband was always easiest with some cake in his belly.

"It might be our last chance to bag us some fresh organs," Velvet said. "Do you know how much they go for on the market these days?"

"Yeah, it's crazy," Pora said. "But I'm not sure I can make it next weekend."

"Come on, you know you want to," Velvet said. "You're the second best hunter in the neighborhood."

"Second best?"

Velvet laughed. "Well, you're a good shot, but nobody's better than me."

Pora laughed at her.

"I might have to watch the kids next weekend," she said.

"Bring them along," Velvet cried. "They're boys. Boys love a good human hunt."

"I'll get back to you on that," Pora said. "If Poro doesn't have a heart attack once I lay this news on him, he might be okay with letting me go on a little hunting trip."

"Well, good luck with that, Pandy," Velvet said. "Love you."

"Love you too, Bunny," Pora said.

When she hung up the phone, Pora realized she had smooshed her belly into the cake when she wasn't paying attention, coating her stomach in chocolate frosting and the cake in a layer of white fuzz.

Pora took her daughter and two sons to the toy shop to celebrate her new pregnancy.

"We can have any toy we want?" asked Pete, her youngest child. His black fuzzy eyes lit up with excitement.

"Anything you want," Pora said.

The three fluffy children ran wild through the store, grabbing at everything they came across. Pora just sat by the front counter, smiling at their liveliness. Seeing them happy meant everything in the world to her, even if she had to spoil them every now and then. Although her husband was in a shady line of work that had gotten him into trouble with the law more than a few times, he brought home a lot of money. And Pora liked spending his money on her children.

"Are those smart-toys?" Pora asked the clerk, as she saw what kind of toys her children were looking through.

The toy shop clerk was a big gray stuffed animal with long scraggly hair. He was supposed to be a wolf but looked more like a Scottish deerhound.

"Ah yes," said the clerk. "Those toys are top of the line. They can walk and talk and play with your child. It's like they're really alive."

"Oh, wow," Pora said. "That sounds amazing."

The clerk pulled out a display model. It was a little koala bear that marched along the counter and held out its arms to be hugged.

"Momma?" said the toy koala.

"Oh, how cute," Pora said.

"And they're a hundred percent safe," said the clerk. "As long as you show them love, they'll love you back."

Pora saw a toy dog on a dusty shelf behind the counter.

"What's that one?" she asked the clerk. "I don't think I've seen that kind of toy before."

"Oh, that," said the clerk. "That's an old model of toy. They don't make anything like these anymore."

"Why's that?"

The clerk took the large plastic dog off the shelf and placed it on the counter. It was designed to look like a poodle, but its casing was silver and gold. It was like a robot dog.

"It's one of those payback-toys from the early days," said the clerk. "That's when they used to turn human children into toys for our young ones. It was supposed to be like payback for what they did to us."

Pora pointed at the dog.

"So there's a real human inside of there?" she asked.

"Yep," said the clerk. "It's been ten years, but the thing's still alive in there."

"Oh, how fun," Pora said with a smile. Then she looked back at her children. "Hey kids, do you want a payback-toy?" But they were too interested in their smart-toys to listen to her.

"How does it work?" Pora said. "How did they fit a whole human inside of this?"

The clerk lifted the dog upside down and pointed at its belly.

"They chopped it up and dehydrated most of its flesh so that it would shrink up tight," said the clerk. "It's not exactly a living thing anymore, so it doesn't need food and water. It can live on batteries."

"Really?" Pora said.

"The thing could probably live forever if you made sure to change its batteries every few years," said the clerk.

"I can hardly believe it," Pora said. She touched its plastic casing. The thing wasn't moving. It didn't look very alive. "How come it's not doing anything?"

"Oh, yeah," said the clerk. "It's just turned off. When the button is off, it seizes up all of the human's muscles and joints so that it can't move. The *on* button will release them."

The clerk clicked the button and the toy stretched its legs and shook its head. It looked up at Pora with shining electronic eyes. Then the clerk turned it back off and its muscles were frozen in place.

"Neat," Pora said. "How much is it?"

"I'll give it to you half price," said the clerk.

"So cheap?"

"They've been on clearance for a long time. Nobody seems to care about payback anymore. I guess they just want to forget about what happened all those years ago."

"Yeah, I guess so," Pora said.

"So you'll take it?" he asked.

"Sure, why not," she said. "Wrap it up with whatever toys my children pick out."

"Excellent," said the clerk. "I've had this little guy on my shelves for so long I'd thought he'd never sell."

"You caught me at a good time," she said. "I'm in a spending mood today."

The clerk nodded his head excitedly as he packaged up the payback-toy for the panda family. He was happy to finally be rid of the toy. The thing creeped him out. It felt as if it was always staring at him, conspiring to kill him while his back was turned. If Pora hadn't purchased it the clerk probably would have tossed the toy in the garbage by the end of the season.

Back at home, the children ripped open the boxes on their toys and ran upstairs, laughing and screaming.

"Hey, doesn't anyone want to play with the payback-toy?" Pora yelled at them. But they were already up in their rooms.

Pora sighed and sat down on the couch. She placed the toy on the coffee table and stared at its little silver face.

"Don't those kids know anything," she said. "You have to respect your toys. After all our people fought for..."

She clicked the toy's *on* button and waited to see what it could do. The silver dog paused there for a moment. Then it stretched its legs and walked across the table toward her.

"There you go," Pora said, smiling at the walking toy. Then she yelled upstairs, "See kids, this is fun too!"

The toy looked up at the panda with its robot eyes. It opened its mouth as if trying to speak.

"You can speak, too?" Pora asked the toy. "So cute! Say something."

The toy tried to speak but its words couldn't come out.

"Jah," its electronic voice spurted out. "Jah... jah..."

"Huh..." Pora said. "You must be defective."

It continued trying to speak in its high-pitched voice. "Juh... Juuw..."

"What are you trying to say little guy?"

Then it finally got out the word.

"Juuuwleee..." it said.

Pora's fuzzy eyelids narrowed.

"What was that?" she asked.

"Julie," it said again. "Julie..."

Pora leaned back. There was something about that name

that struck a chord in her.

"Who's Julie?" she asked. "Is that your name?"

"Nuh…" it said. "No."

It wagged its whiney tail.

"Yooou are Juuulee," it said. "I ammm Riley."

"Riley?" she asked.

Something was coming to her. Something that she had long forgotten.

"Riley…" she said.

Then, suddenly, she remembered it all. *She* was Julie. She was once human. She remembered her life in the wasteland. She remembered the human prisoner boy named Riley.

She looked down at her hands. The fur was not real. It was grafted onto her human skin.

"You promised," said the toy, its electronic voice crackling. "You promised to get me out."

"Promised?" she asked. She thought about it for a moment. "But Riley died back there. I saw the machines take him apart."

"It's a prison," said the toy. "This body… A prison."

Pora shook her head at the toy.

"I waited for you," it said. "You left me. In prison."

"I'm sorry…"

"In prison."

"I'm sorry," she said. Tears erupted from her eyes. "I don't remember. I don't remember anything."

"Julie…" said the toy. "Kill me."

She put her hand on her mouth.

"Kill me," said the toy. "Free me… From prison."

She reached out her hands and picked the toy off of the table.

"Riley…" she said.

She held it in her lap, looking down on his little face.

"I'm so sorry…" she said.

"Free me…" said the toy.

She wrapped her hands around its neck. Her tears made splatting sounds against its plastic shell.

"Thank you…" said the toy.

As she was about to break the toy's head off, one of her children entered the room.

"Mommy?" asked the boy.

It was Pete, the youngest. When she saw his little face, her head shook as if she had just snapped out of a daze.

She smiled at her boy. "Yes, sweetie?"

Pete came up to Pora and put his little fluffy paw on her knee.

"That toy," he said, pointing at the plastic puppy in her lap. "Is that for me? Can I play with it?"

Pora looked down at the toy.

The toy said, "Free m—"

Its words were cut short as Pora pulled out the wire in its neck, dismantling its voicebox. The toy dog moved its mouth to speak, but its words were silent.

"Of course, honey," Pora said, handing the toy to her child. "I bought it for you. Play with it all you want."

The boy smiled brightly as the toy wiggled its legs in his hands. She watched him run upstairs with his new toy, giggling with delight. His joy filled her heart with a glowing warmth that could not be replaced by anything else.

All she cared about in the world was making her children happy. It was what she lived for.

She placed her hands on her stomach and closed her eyes, imagining all the happiness she would bring to the new baby inside of her. She didn't want to stop at four. She wanted to have seven children, like her sister Velvet. She wanted to do what was right for her people. She wanted to help them multiply.

The glowing smile on her face was still there by the time her husband came home from work. Poro arrived at the door holding flowers.

"Have you been crying?" he asked, as she took the flowers and kissed him on the nose.

"No, of course not," she said, rubbing the water out of her eyes. "Come in the kitchen. I baked you a cake."

"Is it chocolate?" he said, almost singing his words.

"Of course," she said. "Come have some. I've got wonderful news."

She was sure the news wouldn't be quite so wonderful to her husband, but to Pora it was truly the most wonderful news of all.

BONUS SECTION

This is the part of the book where we would have published an afterword by the author but he insisted on drawing a comic strip instead for reasons we don't quite understand.

Thank you for reading my new book, *Cuddly Holocaust.* Wasn't it neato?

It's me CM3!

just finished reading it

WHAT THE FUCK KIND OF ENDING WAS THAT!!

What was with that incest shit? Was it her father's penis or not?

I don't know.

Message?
Hmmm...
Let's see...

Life is complicated.
People are
fucked up...

Especially in
toy apocalypse
world.

*That's not
a message!*

Now he's a
skeleton?

Also it's a metaphor for aging.
People are innocent victims of
society as children,
rebels of society
as teenagers, and
then come to accept
all the fucked up shit
of society as adults.
That was
Julie's arc.

You just made that up this
second didn't you?

Where'd the
bacon strip
band-aid
come from?

Yeah...

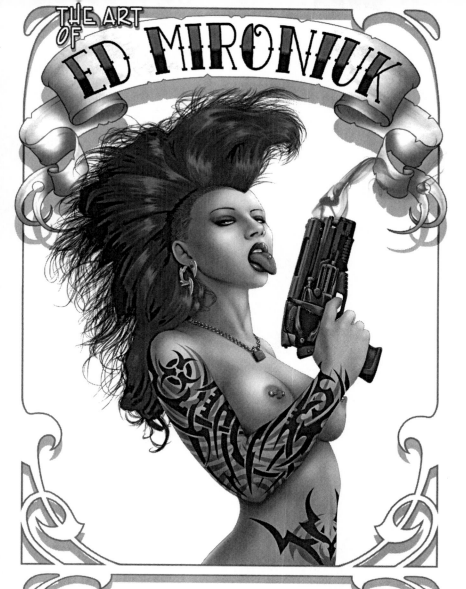

ABOUT THE AUTHOR

Carlton Mellick III is one of the leading authors of the bizarro fiction subgenre. Since 2001, his books have drawn an international cult following, despite the fact that they have been shunned by most libraries and chain bookstores.

He won the Wonderland Book Award for his novel, *Warrior Wolf Women of the Wasteland*, in 2009. His short fiction has appeared in *Vice Magazine, The Year's Best Fantasy and Horror #16, The Magazine of Bizarro Fiction,* and *Zombies: Encounters with the Hungry Dead,* among others. He is also a graduate of Clarion West, where he studied under the likes of Chuck Palahniuk, Connie Willis, and Cory Doctorow.

He lives in Portland, OR, the bizarro fiction mecca.

Visit him online at **www.carltonmellick.com**

BIZARRO BOOKS

CATALOG SPRING 2012

ERASERHEAD PRESS

Your major resource for the bizarro fiction genre:

WWW.BIZARROCENTRAL.COM

Introduce yourselves to the bizarro fiction genre and all of its authors with the Bizarro Starter Kit series. Each volume features short novels and short stories by ten of the leading bizarro authors, designed to give you a perfect sampling of the genre for only $10.

BB-0X1
"The Bizarro Starter Kit" (Orange)

Featuring D. Harlan Wilson, Carlton Mellick III, Jeremy Robert Johnson, Kevin L Donihe, Gina Ranalli, Andre Duza, Vincent W. Sakowski, Steve Beard, John Edward Lawson, and Bruce Taylor. **236 pages $10**

BB-0X2
"The Bizarro Starter Kit" (Blue)

Featuring Ray Fracalossy, Jeremy C. Shipp, Jordan Krall, Mykle Hansen, Andersen Prunty, Eckhard Gerdes, Bradley Sands, Steve Aylett, Christian TeBordo, and Tony Rauch. **244 pages $10**

BB-0X2
"The Bizarro Starter Kit" (Purple)

Featuring Russell Edson, Athena Villaverde, David Agranoff, Matthew Revert, Andrew Goldfarb, Jeff Burk, Garrett Cook, Kris Saknussemm, Cody Goodfellow, and Cameron Pierce **264 pages $10**

BB-001 "The Kafka Effekt" D. Harlan Wilson — A collection of forty-four irreal short stories loosely written in the vein of Franz Kafka, with more than a pinch of William S. Burroughs sprinkled on top. **211 pages $14**

BB-002 "Satan Burger" Carlton Mellick III — The cult novel that put Carlton Mellick III on the map ... Six punks get jobs at a fast food restaurant owned by the devil in a city violently overpopulated by surreal alien cultures. **236 pages $14**

BB-003 "Some Things Are Better Left Unplugged" Vincent Sakwoski — Join The Man and his Nemesis, the obese tabby, for a nightmare roller coaster ride into this postmodern fantasy. **152 pages $10**

BB-004 "Shall We Gather At the Garden?" Kevin L Donihe — Donihe's Debut novel. Midgets take over the world, The Church of Lionel Richie vs. The Church of the Byrds, plant porn and more! **244 pages $14**

BB-005 "Razor Wire Pubic Hair" Carlton Mellick III — A genderless humandildo is purchased by a razor dominatrix and brought into her nightmarish world of bizarre sex and mutilation. **176 pages $11**

BB-006 "Stranger on the Loose" D. Harlan Wilson — The fiction of Wilson's 2nd collection is planted in the soil of normalcy, but what grows out of that soil is a dark, witty, otherworldly jungle... **228 pages $14**

BB-007 "The Baby Jesus Butt Plug" Carlton Mellick III — Using clones of the Baby Jesus for anal sex will be the hip sex fetish of the future. **92 pages $10**

BB-008 "Fishyfleshed" Carlton Mellick III — The world of the past is an illogical flatland lacking in dimension and color, a sick-scape of crispy squid people wandering the desert for no apparent reason. **260 pages $14**

BB-009 **"Dead Bitch Army" Andre Duza** — Step into a world filled with racist teenagers, cannibals, 100 warped Uncle Sams, automobiles with razor-sharp teeth, living graffiti, and a pissed-off zombie bitch out for revenge. **344 pages $16**

BB-010 **"The Menstruating Mall" Carlton Mellick III** — "The Breakfast Club meets Chopping Mall as directed by David Lynch." - Brian Keene **212 pages $12**

BB-011 **"Angel Dust Apocalypse" Jeremy Robert Johnson** — Meth-heads, man-made monsters, and murderous Neo-Nazis. "Seriously amazing short stories..." - Chuck Palahniuk, author of Fight Club **184 pages $11**

BB-012 **"Ocean of Lard" Kevin L Donihe / Carlton Mellick III** — A parody of those old Choose Your Own Adventure kid's books about some very odd pirates sailing on a sea made of animal fat. **176 pages $12**

BB-015 **"Foop!" Chris Genoa** — Strange happenings are going on at Dactyl, Inc, the world's first and only time travel tourism company.
"A surreal pie in the face!" - Christopher Moore **300 pages $14**

BB-020 **"Punk Land" Carlton Mellick III** — In the punk version of Heaven, the anarchist utopia is threatened by corporate fascism and only Goblin, Mortician's sperm, and a blue-mohawked female assassin named Shark Girl can stop them. **284 pages $15**

BB-027 **"Siren Promised" Jeremy Robert Johnson & Alan M Clark** — Nominated for the Bram Stoker Award. A potent mix of bad drugs, bad dreams, brutal bad guys, and surreal/incredible art by Alan M. Clark. **190 pages $13**

BB-031 **"Sea of the Patchwork Cats" Carlton Mellick III** — A quiet dreamlike tale set in the ashes of the human race. For Mellick enthusiasts who also adore The Twilight Zone. **112 pages $10**

BB-032 "Extinction Journals" Jeremy Robert Johnson — An uncanny voyage across a newly nuclear America where one man must confront the problems associated with loneliness, insane dieties, radiation, love, and an ever-evolving cockroach suit with a mind of its own. **104 pages $10**

BB-037 "The Haunted Vagina" Carlton Mellick III — It's difficult to love a woman whose vagina is a gateway to the world of the dead. **132 pages $10**

BB-043 "War Slut"   Carlton Mellick III — Part "1984," part "Waiting for Godot," and part action horror video game adaptation of John Carpenter's "The Thing." **116 pages $10**

BB-047 "Sausagey Santa" Carlton Mellick III — A bizarro Christmas tale featuring Santa as a piratey mutant with a body made of sausages. 124 pages $10

BB-048 "Misadventures in a Thumbnail Universe" Vincent Sakowski — Dive deep into the surreal and satirical realms of neo-classical Blender Fiction, filled with television shoes and flesh-filled skies. **120 pages $10**

BB-053 "Ballad of a Slow Poisoner" Andrew Goldfarb — Millford Mutterwurst sat down on a Tuesday to take his afternoon tea, and made the unpleasant discovery that his elbows were becoming flatter. **128 pages $10**

BB-055 "Help! A Bear is Eating Me" Mykle Hansen — The bizarro, heartwarming, magical tale of poor planning, hubris and severe blood loss...
150 pages $11

BB-056 "Piecemeal June" Jordan Krall — A man falls in love with a living sex doll, but with love comes danger when her creator comes after her with crab-squid assassins. **90 pages $9**

BB-058 "The Overwhelming Urge" Andersen Prunty — A collection of bizarro tales by Andersen Prunty. **150 pages $11**

BB-059 "Adolf in Wonderland" Carlton Mellick III — A dreamlike adventure that takes a young descendant of Adolf Hitler's design and sends him down the rabbit hole into a world of imperfection and disorder. **180 pages $11**

BB-061 "Ultra Fuckers" Carlton Mellick III — Absurdist suburban horror about a couple who enter an upper middle class gated community but can't find their way out. **108 pages $9**

BB-062 "House of Houses" Kevin L. Donihe — An odd man wants to marry his house. Unfortunately, all of the houses in the world collapse at the same time in the Great House Holocaust. Now he must travel to House Heaven to find his departed fiancee. **172 pages $11**

BB-064 "Squid Pulp Blues" Jordan Krall — In these three bizarro-noir novellas, the reader is thrown into a world of murderers, drugs made from squid parts, deformed gun-toting veterans, and a mischievous apocalyptic donkey. **204 pages $12**

BB-065 "Jack and Mr. Grin" Andersen Prunty — "When Mr. Grin calls you can hear a smile in his voice. Not a warm and friendly smile, but the kind that seizes your spine in fear. You don't need to pay your phone bill to hear it. That smile is in every line of Prunty's prose." - Tom Bradley. **208 pages $12**

BB-066 "Cybernetrix" Carlton Mellick III — What would you do if your normal everyday world was slowly mutating into the video game world from Tron? **212 pages $12**

BB-072 "Zerostrata" Andersen Prunty — Hansel Nothing lives in a tree house, suffers from memory loss, has a very eccentric family, and falls in love with a woman who runs naked through the woods every night. **144 pages $11**

BB-073 "The Egg Man" Carlton Mellick III — It is a world where humans reproduce like insects. Children are the property of corporations, and having an enormous ten-foot brain implanted into your skull is a grotesque sexual fetish. Mellick's industrial urban dystopia is one of his darkest and grittiest to date. **184 pages $11**

BB-074 "Shark Hunting in Paradise Garden" Cameron Pierce — A group of strange humanoid religious fanatics travel back in time to the Garden of Eden to discover it is invested with hundreds of giant flying maneating sharks. **150 pages $10**

BB-075 "Apeshit" Carlton Mellick III - Friday the 13th meets Visitor Q. Six hipster teens go to a cabin in the woods inhabited by a deformed killer. An incredibly fucked-up parody of B-horror movies with a bizarro slant. **192 pages $12**

BB-076 "Fuckers of Everything on the Crazy Shitting Planet of the Vomit At smosphere" Mykle Hansen - Three bizarro satires. Monster Cocks, Journey to the Center of Agnes Cuddlebottom, and Crazy Shitting Planet. **228 pages $12**

BB-077 "The Kissing Bug" Daniel Scott Buck — In the tradition of Roald Dahl, Tim Burton, and Edward Gorey, comes this bizarro anti-war children's story about a bohemian conenose kissing bug who falls in love with a human woman. **116 pages $10**

BB-078 "MachoPoni" Lotus Rose — It's My Little Pony... *Bizarro* style! A long time ago Poniworld was split in two. On one side of the Jagged Line is the Pastel Kingdom, a magical land of music, parties, and positivity. On the other side of the Jagged Line is Dark Kingdom inhabited by an army of undead ponies. **148 pages $11**

BB-079 "The Faggiest Vampire" Carlton Mellick III — A Roald Dahl-esque children's story about two faggy vampires who partake in a mustache competition to find out which one is truly the faggiest. **104 pages $10**

BB-080 "Sky Tongues" Gina Ranalli — The autobiography of Sky Tongues, the biracial hermaphrodite actress with tongues for fingers. Follow her strange life story as she rises from freak to fame. **204 pages $12**

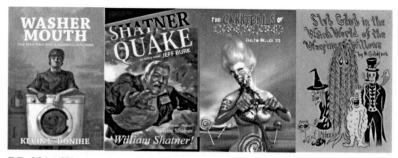

BB-081 **"Washer Mouth" Kevin L. Donihe** - A washing machine becomes human and pursues his dream of meeting his favorite soap opera star. **244 pages $11**

BB-082 **"Shatnerquake" Jeff Burk** - All of the characters ever played by William Shatner are suddenly sucked into our world. Their mission: hunt down and destroy the real William Shatner. **100 pages $10**

BB-083 **"The Cannibals of Candyland" Carlton Mellick III** - There exists a race of cannibals that are made of candy. They live in an underground world made out of candy. One man has dedicated his life to killing them all. **170 pages $11**

BB-084 **"Slub Glub in the Weird World of the Weeping Willows" Andrew Goldfarb** - The charming tale of a blue glob named Slub Glub who helps the weeping willows whose tears are flooding the earth. There are also hyenas, ghosts, and a voodoo priest **100 pages $10**

BB-085 **"Super Fetus" Adam Pepper** - Try to abort this fetus and he'll kick your ass! **104 pages $10**

BB-086 **"Fistful of Feet" Jordan Krall** - A bizarro tribute to spaghetti westerns, featuring Cthulhu-worshipping Indians, a woman with four feet, a crazed gunman who is obsessed with sucking on candy, Syphilis-ridden mutants, sexually transmitted tattoos, and a house devoted to the freakiest fetishes. **228 pages $12**

BB-087 **"Ass Goblins of Auschwitz" Cameron Pierce** - It's Monty Python meets Nazi exploitation in a surreal nightmare as can only be imagined by Bizarro author Cameron Pierce. **104 pages $10**

BB-088 **"Silent Weapons for Quiet Wars" Cody Goodfellow** - "This is high-end psychological surrealist horror meets bottom-feeding low-life crime in a techno-thrilling science fiction world full of Lovecraft and magic..." -John Skipp **212 pages $12**

BB-089 "Warrior Wolf Women of the Wasteland" Carlton Mellick III
— Road Warrior Werewolves versus McDonaldland Mutants...post-apocalyptic fiction has never been quite like this. **316 pages $13**

BB-091 "Super Giant Monster Time" Jeff Burk — A tribute to choose your own adventures and Godzilla movies. Will you escape the giant monsters that are rampaging the fuck out of your city and shit? Or will you join the mob of alien-controlled punk rockers causing chaos in the streets? What happens next depends on you. **188 pages $12**

BB-092 "Perfect Union" Cody Goodfellow — "Cronenberg's THE FLY on a grand scale: human/insect gene-spliced body horror, where the human hive politics are as shocking as the gore." -John Skipp. **272 pages $13**

BB-093 "Sunset with a Beard" Carlton Mellick III — 14 stories of surreal science fiction. **200 pages $12**

BB-094 "My Fake War" Andersen Prunty — The absurd tale of an unlikely soldier forced to fight a war that, quite possibly, does not exist. It's Rambo meets Waiting for Godot in this subversive satire of American values and the scope of the human imagination. **128 pages $11**

BB-095 "Lost in Cat Brain Land" Cameron Pierce — Sad stories from a surreal world. A fascist mustache, the ghost of Franz Kafka, a desert inside a dead cat. Primordial entities mourn the death of their child. The desperate serve tea to mysterious creatures. A hopeless romantic falls in love with a pterodactyl. And much more. **152 pages $11**

BB-096 "The Kobold Wizard's Dildo of Enlightenment +2" Carlton Mellick III — A Dungeons and Dragons parody about a group of people who learn they are only made up characters in an AD&D campaign and must find a way to resist their nerdy teenaged players and retarded dungeon master in order to survive. 232 **pages $12**

BB-098 "A Hundred Horrible Sorrows of Ogner Stump" Andrew Goldfarb — Goldfarb's acclaimed comic series. A magical and weird journey into the horrors of everyday life. **164 pages $11**

BB-099 "Pickled Apocalypse of Pancake Island" Cameron Pierce—A demented fairy tale about a pickle, a pancake, and the apocalypse. **102 pages $8**

BB-100 "Slag Attack" Andersen Prunty— Slag Attack features four visceral, noir stories about the living, crawling apocalypse.A slag is what survivors are calling the slug-like maggots raining from the sky, burrowing inside people, and hollowing out their flesh and their sanity. **148 pages $11**

BB-101 "Slaughterhouse High" Robert Devereaux—A place where schools are built with secret passageways, rebellious teens get zippers installed in their mouths and genitals, and once a year, on that special night, one couple is slaughtered and the bits of their bodies are kept as souvenirs. **304 pages $13**

BB-102 "The Emerald Burrito of Oz" John Skipp & Marc Levinthal—OZ IS REAL! Magic is real! The gate is really in Kansas! And America is finally allowing Earth tourists to visit this weird-ass, mysterious land. But when Gene of Los Angeles heads off for summer vacation in the Emerald City, little does he know that a war is brewing...a war that could destroy both worlds. **280 pages $13**

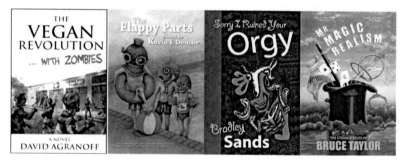

BB-103 "The Vegan Revolution... with Zombies" David Agranoff—When there's no more meat in hell, the vegans will walk the earth. **160 pages $11**

BB-104 "The Flappy Parts" Kevin L Donihe—Poems about bunnies, LSD, and police abuse. You know, things that matter. 132 **pages $11**

BB-105 "Sorry I Ruined Your Orgy" Bradley Sands—Bizarro humorist Bradley Sands returns with one of the strangest, most hilarious collections of the year. **130 pages $11**

BB-106 "Mr. Magic Realism" Bruce Taylor—Like Golden Age science fiction comics written by Freud, *Mr. Magic Realism* is a strange, insightful adventure that spans the furthest reaches of the galaxy, exploring the hidden caverns in the hearts and minds of men, women, aliens, and biomechanical cats. **152 pages $11**

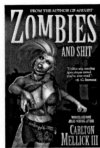

BB-107 **"Zombies and Shit" Carlton Mellick III**—"Battle Royale" meets "Return of the Living Dead." Mellick's bizarro tribute to the zombie genre. **308 pages $13**

BB-108 **"The Cannibal's Guide to Ethical Living" Mykle Hansen**—Over a five star French meal of fine wine, organic vegetables and human flesh, a lunatic delivers a witty, chilling, disturbingly sane argument in favor of eating the rich.. **184 pages $11**

BB-109 **"Starfish Girl" Athena Villaverde**—In a post-apocalyptic underwater dome society, a girl with a starfish growing from her head and an assassin with sea anenome hair are on the run from a gang of mutant fish men. **160 pages $11**

BB-110 **"Lick Your Neighbor" Chris Genoa**—Mutant ninjas, a talking whale, kung fu masters, maniacal pilgrims, and an alcoholic clown populate Chris Genoa's surreal, darkly comical and unnerving reimagining of the first Thanksgiving. **303 pages $13**

BB-111 **"Night of the Assholes" Kevin L. Donihe**—A plague of assholes is infecting the countryside. Normal everyday people are transforming into jerks, snobs, dicks, and douchebags. And they all have only one purpose: to make your life a living hell.. **192 pages $11**

BB-112 **"Jimmy Plush, Teddy Bear Detective" Garrett Cook**—Hardboiled cases of a private detective trapped within a teddy bear body. **180 pages $11**

BB-113 **"The Deadheart Shelters" Forrest Armstrong**—The hip hop lovechild of William Burroughs and Dali... **144 pages $11**

BB-114 **"Eyeballs Growing All Over Me... Again" Tony Raugh**—Absurd, surreal, playful, dream-like, whimsical, and a lot of fun to read. **144 pages $11**

BB-115 **"Whargoul" Dave Brockie** — From the killing grounds of Stalingrad to the death camps of the holocaust. From torture chambers in Iraq to race riots in the United States, the Whargoul was there, killing and raping. **244 pages $12**

BB-116 **"By the Time We Leave Here, We'll Be Friends" J. David Osborne** — A David Lynchian nightmare set in a Russian gulag, where its prisoners, guards, traitors, soldiers, lovers, and demons fight for survival and their own rapidly deteriorating humanity. **168 pages $11**

BB-117 **"Christmas on Crack" edited by Carlton Mellick III** — Perverted Christmas Tales for the whole family! . . . as long as every member of your family is over the age of 18. **168 pages $11**

BB-118 **"Crab Town" Carlton Mellick III** — Radiation fetishists, balloon people, mutant crabs, sail-bike road warriors, and a love affair between a woman and an H-Bomb. This is one mean asshole of a city. Welcome to Crab Town. **100 pages $8**

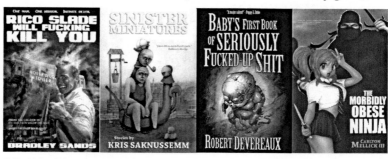

BB-119 **"Rico Slade Will Fucking Kill You" Bradley Sands** — Rico Slade is an action hero. Rico Slade can rip out a throat with his bare hands. Rico Slade's favorite food is the honey-roasted peanut. Rico Slade will fucking kill everyone. A novel. **122 pages $8**

BB-120 **"Sinister Miniatures" Kris Saknussemm** — The definitive collection of short fiction by Kris Saknussemm, confirming that he is one of the best, most daring writers of the weird to emerge in the twenty-first century. **180 pages $11**

BB-121 **"Baby's First Book of Seriously Fucked up Shit" Robert Devereaux** — Ten stories of the strange, the gross, and the just plain fucked up from one of the most original voices in horror. **176 pages $11**

BB-122 **"The Morbidly Obese Ninja" Carlton Mellick III** — These days, if you want to run a successful company . . . you're going to need a lot of ninjas. **92 pages $8**

BB-123 **"Abortion Arcade" Cameron Pierce** — An intoxicating blend of body horror and midnight movie madness, reminiscent of early David Lynch and the splatterpunks at their most sublime. **172 pages $11**

BB-124 **"Black Hole Blues" Patrick Wensink** — A hilarious double helix of country music and physics. **196 pages $11**

BB-125 **"Barbarian Beast Bitches of the Badlands" Carlton Mellick III** — Three prequels and sequels to *Warrior Wolf Women of the Wasteland*. **284 pages $13**

BB-126 **"The Traveling Dildo Salesman" Kevin L. Donihe** — A nightmare comedy about destiny, faith, and sex toys. Also featuring Donihe's most lurid and infamous short stories: *Milky Agitation, Two-Way Santa, The Helen Mower, Living Room Zombies*, and *Revenge of the Living Masturbation Rag.* **108 pages $8**

BB-127 **"Metamorphosis Blues" Bruce Taylor** — Enter a land of love beasts, intergalactic cowboys, and rock 'n roll. A land where Sears Catalogs are doorways to insanity and men keep mysterious black boxes. Welcome to the monstrous mind of Mr. Magic Realism. **136 pages $11**

BB-128 **"The Driver's Guide to Hitting Pedestrians" Andersen Prunty** — A pocket guide to the twenty-three most painful things in life, written by the most well-adjusted man in the universe. **108 pages $8**

BB-129 **"Island of the Super People" Kevin Shamel** — Four students and their anthropology professor journey to a remote island to study its indigenous population. But this is no ordinary native culture. They're super heroes and villains with flesh costumes and out-landish abilities like self-detonation, musical eyelashes, and microwave hands. **194 pages $11**

BB-130 **"Fantastic Orgy" Carlton Mellick III** — Shark Sex, mutant cats, and strange sexually transmitted diseases. Featuring the stories: *Candy-coated, Ear Cat, Fantastic Orgy, City Hobgoblins*, and *Porno in August.* **136 pages $9**

BB-131 "Cripple Wolf" Jeff Burk — Part man. Part wolf. 100% crippled. Also including *Punk Rock Nursing Home, Adrift with Space Badgers, Cook for Your Life, Just Another Day in the Park, Frosty and the Full Monty,* and *House of Cats.* **152 pages $10**

BB-132 "I Knocked Up Satan's Daughter" Carlton Mellick III — An adorable, violent, fantastical love story. A romantic comedy for the bizarro fiction reader. **152 pages $10**

BB-133 "A Town Called Suckhole" David W. Barbee — Far into the future, in the nuclear bowels of post-apocalyptic Dixie, there is a town. A town of derelict mobile homes, ancient junk, and mutant wildlife. A town of slack jawed rednecks who bask in the splendors of moonshine and mud boggin'. A town dedicated to the bloody and demented legacy of the Old South. A town called Suckhole. **144 pages $10**

BB-134 "Cthulhu Comes to the Vampire Kingdom" Cameron Pierce — What you'd get if H. P. Lovecraft wrote a Tim Burton animated film. **148 pages $11**

BB-135 "I am Genghis Cum" Violet LeVoit — From the savage Arctic tundra to post-partum mutations to your missing daughter's unmarked grave, join visionary madwoman Violet LeVoit in this non-stop eight-story onslaught of full-tilt Bizarro punk lit thrills. **124 pages $9**

BB-136 "Haunt" Laura Lee Bahr — A tripping-balls Los Angeles noir, where a mysterious dame drags you through a time-warping Bizarro hall of mirrors. **316 pages $13**

BB-137 "Amazing Stories of the Flying Spaghetti Monster" edited by Cameron Pierce — Like an all-spaghetti evening of Adult Swim, the Flying Spaghetti Monster will show you the many realms of His Noodly Appendage. Learn of those who worship him and the lives he touches in distant, mysterious ways. **228 pages $12**

BB-138 "Wave of Mutilation" Douglas Lain — A dream-pop exploration of modern architecture and the American identity, *Wave of Mutilation* is a Zen finger trap for the 21st century. **100 pages $8**

BB-139 **"Hooray for Death!" Mykle Hansen** — Famous Author Mykle Hansen draws unconventional humor from deaths tiny and large, and invites you to laugh while you can. **128 pages $10**

BB-140 **"Hypno-hog's Moonshine Monster Jamboree" Andrew Goldfarb** — Hicks, Hogs, Horror! Goldfarb is back with another strange illustrated tale of backwoods weirdness. **120 pages $9**

BB-141 **"Broken Piano For President" Patrick Wensink** — A comic masterpiece about the fast food industry, booze, and the necessity to choose happiness over work and security. **372 pages $15**

BB-142 **"Please Do Not Shoot Me in the Face" Bradley Sands** — A novel in three parts, *Please Do Not Shoot Me in the Face: A Novel*, is the story of one boy detective, the worst ninja in the world, and the great American fast food wars. It is a novel of loss, destruction, and--incredibly--genuine hope. **224 pages $12**

BB-143 **"Santa Steps Out" Robert Devereaux** — Sex, Death, and Santa Claus ... The ultimate erotic Christmas story is back. **294 pages $13**

BB-144 **"Santa Conquers the Homophobes" Robert Devereaux** — "I wish I could hope to ever attain one-thousandth the perversity of Robert Devereaux's toenail clippings." - Poppy Z. Brite **316 pages $13**

BB-145 **"We Live Inside You" Jeremy Robert Johnson** — "Jeremy Robert Johnson is dancing to a way different drummer. He loves language, he loves the edge, and he loves us people. These stories have range and style and wit. This is entertainment... and literature."- Jack Ketchum **188 pages $11**

BB-146 **"Clockwork Girl" Athena Villaverde** — Urban fairy tales for the weird girl in all of us. Like a combination of Francesca Lia Block, Charles de Lint, Kathe Koja, Tim Burton, and Hayao Miyazaki, her stories are cute, kinky, edgy, magical, provocative, and strange, full of poetic imagery and vicious sexuality. **160 pages $10**

BB-147 "Armadillo Fists" Carlton Mellick III — A weird-as-hell gangster story set in a world where people drive giant mechanical dinosaurs instead of cars. **168 pages $11**

BB-148 "Gargoyle Girls of Spider Island" Cameron Pierce — Four college seniors venture out into open waters for the tropical party weekend of a lifetime. Instead of a teenage sex fantasy, they find themselves in a nightmare of pirates, sharks, and sex-crazed monsters. **100 pages $8**

BB-149 "The Handsome Squirm" by Carlton Mellick III — Like Franz Kafka's *The Trial* meets an erotic body horror version of *The Blob*. **158 pages $11**

BB-150 "Tentacle Death Trip" Jordan Krall — It's *Death Race 2000* meets H. P. Lovecraft in bizarro author Jordan Krall's best and most suspenseful work to date. **224 pages $12**

BB-151 "The Obese" Nick Antosca — Like Alfred Hitchcock's *The Birds*... but with obese people. **108 pages $10**

BB-152 "All-Monster Action!" Cody Goodfellow — The world gave him a blank check and a demand: Create giant monsters to fight our wars. But Dr. Otaku was not satisfied with mere chaos and mass destruction.... **216 pages $12**

BB-153 "Ugly Heaven" Carlton Mellick III — Heaven is no longer a paradise. It was once a blissful utopia full of wonders far beyond human comprehension. But the afterlife is now in ruins. It has become an ugly, lonely wasteland populated by strange monstrous beasts, masturbating angels, and sad man-like beings wallowing in the remains of the once-great Kingdom of God. **106 pages $8**

BB-154 "Space Walrus" Kevin L. Donihe — Walter is supposed to go where no walrus has ever gone before, but all this astronaut walrus really wants is to take it easy on the intense training, escape the chimpanzee bullies, and win the love of his human trainer Dr. Stephanie. **160 pages $11**

Lightning Source UK Ltd.
Milton Keynes UK
UKOW02f1859250716

279216UK00001B/35/P